CUENTOS: FROM THE SOUTH TO THE CITY

Keiarra Ortiz-Cedeno

ISBN-9798993511900

Cover design by: Art Painter
Library of Congress Control Number: 2018675309
Printed in the United States of America

Thank you most of all to my mother, who, since my earliest days, has always stressed the importance of reading and writing. Thank you also to Ms. Brown for helping me find my voice. I wish you could have seen this book. I am forever grateful to my friends and family who have supported me along the way. I wouldn't be here without you.

CONTENTS

CHAPTER 1

Before the first blue-gold suggestion of sunrise can pierce the sky over Texarkana, Mary Lee Payton has already parted the night with her own keys, a precise clatter at the dark glass door of the laundromat. She is nothing if not diligent, for what is diligence but a breed of faith.

The fluorescent lights snap on with a stubborn delay, flickering in uneven intervals, each bulb shuddering toward life and then succumbing, with an audible click, to the next. The effect is strobe-like, and in these brief throbs of pallid light the true condition of the floor becomes visible: a scuffed parade of tracks, patched in places where time has worn through the original promise of shine. Mary Lee surveys her kingdom with a pursed mouth.

She circles the perimeter, adjusting the blinds with a hasty, practiced twitch, then running a hand over the pitted metal of each machine as though they were livestock to be fed, readied, kept alive for labor. She checks coin slots for jammed pennies, the treacherous foreign currency of children and the desperate. Each machine is hers by right of vigilance, and she knows which have a history of stalling, which ones need a hip-check to initiate the cycle, and which can be trusted to run without supervision. At the rear wall, she bends with unexpected grace to open the change dispenser, inventorying quarters and dimes, counting them against her own ledger, neat as a pin. She finds satisfaction not in the weight of money, but in its absolute predictability. The safe under the counter is checked twice—latch, code, contents

—before she allows herself to arrange the powder boxes in their wire rack, each label facing out as if the soap might judge her otherwise.

There is always a lull, a short eternity, between preparation and the arrival of the girls. Mary Lee treasures this, the only stretch of minutes in the day when she might belong entirely to herself. In this interval she sits at the counter, spine rigid against the plastic seat, and gazes through the streaked plate glass at the world she knows better than her own pulse. Across the street, a sagging porch hosts a clutch of feral cats, their fur shining with oil from the fish market's dumpsters. Beyond, the spindled arms of the water tower scrape the lowering clouds, and further still, the brick-red gable of the colored church floats above the mist like a benediction, or a threat. The street itself is a rut of clay and gravel, the curbs trailing down into ditches choked with last year's paper and the spring's new weedlings. All of this belongs to the morning, before the world remembers itself.

When Tara arrives, her approach is marked by a kind of careful exuberance. She opens the door with a forceful swing—never a child's tentativeness, always as though daring the hinges to resist her. She is in her third-best dress, one reserved for work, but manages even in this to look as if she's dressed for an occasion. Her shoes are clean, heels practical but trimmed with a single line of patent black. Her hair is tucked in a scarf—pale yellow, tied low at the nape. She moves with a brightness that at first seems borrowed from a finer home, but on closer inspection is forged from the same stern material as her mother's will.

"Morning, Mama," she sings, setting her book bag on the counter, and not waiting for permission to slip behind it. She opens the ledger and fans through the pages, eyes moving line to line with an eagerness sharpened by years of being watched for error.

Mary Lee nods, not needing to return the greeting. Instead, she offers the first instruction of the day: "You run through the register tape from yesterday?"

Tara, already poised with pencil, lifts her chin. "Balanced last night before I locked up. Only off by seven cents, and I fixed it this morning." She raises the tape as proof, thumb pinned on the final tally.

"Good," Mary Lee says, voice almost warm.

Next comes Beth, trailing the day behind her as if it were a chain or a shroud. Her skin is several shades darker than Tara's —a reminder Mary Lee never needed of the man who'd left her pregnant and unmarried at seventeen. Beth wears her hair loose, falling past her shoulders in an unruly cloud that no one dares remark on anymore. Her dress is plain, navy blue, the hem falling a little too long for ease—another hand-me-down, unlike the carefully tailored dresses Mary Lee sews for Tara, last keepsakes from a husband who'd returned from war in a flag-draped box. Beth's entrance is soft, not in the manner of someone who fears intrusion, but with the resignation of a child who learned early that her presence would never be celebrated like her half-sister's.

She glances once at her mother, then at Tara, then lets her eyes drop to the bucket and mop in the back corner. Without waiting for a word, she moves toward her task.

"Tara, you run the front. Beth, get those utility sinks and the floor in back." Mary Lee speaks not as an instructor but as the conductor of a symphony she wrote herself. "Be sure to scrub around the drains. Last week's bleach left a ring."

Beth doesn't answer, but she doesn't need to. The answer is in the set of her jaw, the careful way she pours the powder, the quickness of her hands in filling the bucket. Her knuckles are already scarred from detergent burns, but she wears them as a distinction—proof of having worked, and survived, in the family line.

By six a.m., the air inside the laundromat is already humid, heavy with the sweet and slightly acrid scent of soap. The first customers drift in—mostly women, all Black, many with children in tow. They greet Mary Lee with a respect that borders on deference. She is both a fixture and a force in the neighborhood, her reputation woven into the fabric of their lives. The men arrive later, usually to fetch or carry, seldom to linger.

Mary Lee presides over it all, shifting between tasks with the efficiency of someone who has never trusted anyone else to do a thing right. She keeps a running log of every load, every exchange, and every time a customer seems slow to count change. The soundscape is percussive: coins clattering in machines, water sluicing through hoses, the rubber slap of sneakers on linoleum, and always—always—the murmur of voices, rising and falling in waves.

In a lull between customers, Mary Lee turns her gaze to the street, where the sky is just now bleeding into a dull gray. She notes the pale streaks of fog that curl around the church steeple, and the way the morning's light divides the town, half in gold and half in shadow. It is a small thing, but Mary Lee records the observation, privately, the way a person might tuck away a bit of string for future use.

Just after seven, the door swings open with an authority rarely seen in their part of town. The woman who enters is not local. She wears a suit the color of eggshell; it nearly matches her skin. Her hair in a severe twist at the crown, and her lipstick a shade that never appears in nature. Her eyes move across the laundromat in a quick sweep, then settle on Tara, who stands at the counter, ledger in hand, smile carefully composed.

"Excuse me," the woman says, loud enough to command the attention of every person in the room. "Is this place open to the public, or is it private?" Her accent is not from Texas, and certainly not from this part of Arkansas. The vowels are clipped, the consonants bitten off as if to spare them the indignity of lingering in the air.

Mary Lee does not move, but a shift passes through her body—a tightening, as though bracing for impact. She lifts her chin and calls, "Tara, help the lady."

Tara places the ledger on the counter, folds her hands with a small and practiced grace, and walks to the front. "We're open," she says, smile unwavering. "If you need change, I can help you at the register."

The woman's eyes appraise Tara, pausing on her skin, the delicate arch of her brow, the unmistakable clarity of her voice. "You folks run this place?" the woman asks, with a pointed look at the machines and the women who tend them.

Mary Lee walks forward then, joining Tara at the counter, and sets her hand firmly on the surface, knuckles whitening.

"We do," she answers, the words measured, each vowel weighed for the risk it carries. "It's our family's business. Been here ten years now."

The woman considers this. "I see," she says, but her tone suggests otherwise. She hands a ten-dollar bill to Tara with a gesture that is almost an afterthought. "I'll need quarters, then."

Tara makes the change, her fingers never trembling, and hands back the stack of coins with a polite, "Let us know if you need help with the machines." The transaction is over, but the woman lingers, her gaze passing back and forth between mother and daughter as if trying to decipher a secret code.

Beth, watching from the back room, resumes her mopping, but her strokes are longer now, and a little more violent. She does not miss how her mother's posture has grown taller, how Tara has squared her shoulders in response. There is a language in the air, one that only the three of them can read.

The white woman chooses a machine as close to the window as possible, and does her washing with an efficiency that borders on hostility. She avoids looking at the others, and when she leaves, the door closes with a finality that will echo in Mary Lee's ears for hours.

The morning resumes, but not as it was before. The regulars re-enter, reclaiming the territory, and the rhythm reasserts itself: the metallic harmony of coins and buttons, the soft, conspiratorial laughter at the folding tables. Yet, in the subtle choreography of the laundromat, something has shifted—some line redrawn, some truth made more visible.

Mary Lee stands at the counter, silent, watching the world beyond the glass as the sun finally hauls itself above the rooftops. In the golden beam that breaks across the linoleum, Tara's hair is limned with a soft glow, and even Beth's mop strokes seem lighter for a moment.

But when the next customer arrives, the roles fall back into place —Tara at the register, Beth at the floor, and Mary Lee watching it all, vigilant as ever. She does not remark on the encounter, nor does she allow her voice to betray any trace of unease. The work continues, because it must, and so do they.

By noon, the laundromat is a bell jar of human heat and suds, the ceiling fans whirring overhead with all the conviction of a politician's promise. It is the Monday rush, which means there is no rush at all—just a steady, crushing continuum of baskets, wet towels, and sticky-fingered children pressed to the glass. The air is soupy, flecked with humidity that settles in the creases behind Beth's knees and welds her dress to the small of her back. She works the mop with the rhythm of a condemned woman, each swipe a testament to the futility of labor against the encroaching tide of sweat and dust.

She is assigned to the rear of the shop today, closest to the great industrial washers, their mouths wide and greedy, always demanding more. The tile here is older, and the grout lines are thick with a kind of historic filth that resists every modern chemical assault. Beth's hands, already marbled with scars, are now pink and raw from the lye and the friction of the mop handle. She watches the veins at her wrists swell with each turn, a blue map of effort that has come to define her.

At the front, Tara is radiant. Not in the way of a pageant girl or movie star, but with a sort of breezy competence that draws every eye. She has a joke for the regulars, an extra moment for the toddlers, and a surgical precision in sorting the bills in the register. The cash drawer never sticks for her; she moves through transactions with the sureness of someone who has never known the sting of doubt. Customers respond accordingly. The old men from the domino hall tip their hats when she calls them "sir." Even the children seem to listen better when Tara is within earshot, as if the cadence of her words has a magnetic pull.

Mary Lee moves between her daughters like a conductor at the edge of a pit orchestra. She walks with the taut, quick steps of a woman whose body can only be trusted so far, and whose mind is already two beats ahead. She corrects Beth's stance at the mop —"You missed that corner again, child, and the drain by the wall needs a soaking"—then turns with equal speed to praise Tara for the crispness of her columns in the ledger book.

"You see, Tara, if you run the numbers as you go, you won't have to fix them later. That's what the big banks do. That's how they keep their heads above water."

Beth bends harder into her task, pushing the mop so far under the line of dryers that her shoulder grinds against the plastic lint trap.

The customers are thick today, all talking at once, their voices floating above the steam like a vapor. Two women near the folding tables are deep in conspiratorial hushes, one with a scarf twisted so tight it notches her jaw. Their eyes dart upward every few words, toward the ceiling. Even if Beth couldn't hear, she would know what the subject was: the second floor and what went on there. The whole neighborhood knew. The room above the laundromat, never spoken of outright, was where men in pressed shirts came with cash folded in their wallets and left with loosened ties. Women in lipstick brighter than daylight arrived through the back entrance, their perfume lingering in the stairwell hours after they'd gone.

Beth had never been allowed up there. The only time she caught a glimpse, the door was ajar and she saw a pale lamp burning above a crimson settee, a half-empty bottle of whiskey, and a woman's silk stocking draped over the arm of a chair. Mary Lee claimed it was storage—just a "spare room for the business." The lie was so bald it circled back to honesty. No one in this part of town could afford spare anything.

The two women by the folding table, emboldened by the din, let their voices rise.
"Heard Charlene made fifty dollars in one night up there last week," one says, eyes cutting toward the register.
"You ask me," the other replies, "it ain't the money. It's the connections. Judge Wilson's car parked out back on a Monday afternoon—that's worth more than cash."

Their laughter is sharp, not cruel but almost proud, a sign of having outlasted something bitter.

Mary Lee shoots them a look that quells the conversation instantly. She does not speak, but her gaze is a blade drawn and left on the table. The women hush, then collect their laundry with unnecessary speed, leaving a faint residue of perfume and gossip in their wake.

At 12:40 sharp, the delivery man arrives. He is not new, but his route is—last week, it was someone older, a man with a limp and a kind word for Beth. This one is young and restless, the type who measures his worth by the pound, by how much he can carry without complaint. He shoulders a box of bleach bottles through the door, grunts, "Supplies for the back," and sets it at Beth's feet.

She kneels to open the carton, slicing the tape with the nail of her thumb. The bleach fumes billow out, singeing her sinuses and making her eyes slick with tears. She does not look up until she hears the slap of a clipboard on the counter.

"Need a signature," the delivery man says, but not to her. Tara, though a good six paces from the register, is already there to take the pen. The man's gaze never touches Beth, not even to mark her as invisible. She watches Tara sign, the loops of her handwriting neat and rounded, and then the brief, courteous exchange that follows: a joke, a smile, the transaction sealed by the touch of fingers over a paper form.

Beth could hate Tara for it, but what she feels is more complicated—a kind of molten embarrassment, as if the man's indifference has seeped into her bloodstream and set up residence there. She wants to throw the mop, to shatter the box of bleach, to make the whole room notice her for the violence of her disappointment. Instead, she stands, wipes her hands on her dress, and returns to scrubbing the floor, her jaw clenched so tight her teeth ache.

The back of the laundromat is a sensory war zone: the slap and gurgle of washers, the bone-white reek of soap, the drone of the steam pressers where Mary Lee smooths the collars of shirts with a surgeon's care. Every sense is assaulted, every movement calculated to produce the maximum result in the least amount of time. Beth finds in this chaos a perverse solace. The more grueling the work, the more it deadens her to everything else. By the time she finishes the floor, her arms are numb, and her mind has retreated to a distant, safer chamber.

She glances at the clock, sees that it is nearly one. The day is only half done, and already the promise of relief has been deferred to some unknowable later. She returns the mop to its corner, straightens her spine, and faces the front. Tara is at the register, chatting with a woman who cradles a baby on one hip. Mary Lee is inspecting the starch delivery, signing off on the manifest with a flourish.

For a moment, Beth stands unseen in the middle of the floor, watching the lines of her family play out in the open like a public performance. She wonders if this is how it will always be: the good daughter in the light, the difficult one in the shadows, and the mother above them both, writing the story as she goes.

She takes a breath and lets it out slow. The hiss of the steam press is almost soothing.

The afternoon wanes by imperceptible degrees, the fluorescents gradually taking over the work of the sun, though nobody would call it an improvement. The crowds have thinned to stragglers, women folding sheets with half the vigor of morning, children asleep on benches or gone to some other place. Even the machines, loyal as they are, seem to slow, their thrum settling into a low mechanical sigh.

Mary Lee claims the counter now, her dominion uncontested in the hush. She counts the register once, then again, her eyes flicking from the bills to Tara's notes in the ledger, as if every decimal is a reflection of character. She narrates the process, a running lesson for Tara, who stands close by, pencil poised, absorbing each correction as both gift and responsibility.

"You see, it's not just about what goes in," Mary Lee intones, tapping a blue-veined finger on the margin, "it's about what you can prove on paper. Never let anyone say you owe more than you can show." Her voice is softer now, nearly indulgent, and in this rare moment she seems almost kind.

Beth knelt in the back corner where Mary Lee always set her, arms moving on automatic over the utility sink. Her stiff brush scraped at the hardened soap residue while bleach fumes stung her nostrils and turned her eyes red. The dull back-and-forth had nearly lulled her into a trance when her mother's voice cracked like a riding crop through the laundromat: "You're staining it!"

Before Beth could even raise her head, Mary Lee's hand snapped down across her backside in a sharp slap. Beth winced, her spine jolting. She gripped the brush tighter, but her elbow jerked upward, striking the bleach bottle perched on the sink's rim. It teetered and fell.

The bottle slid at her feet with a hollow plastic thunk. A gurgle of bleach gushed out, splashing over her shoes, spreading in a pale bloom across the tile, soaking the hem of her dress. The acrid smell clawed at her throat.

Mary Lee loomed over her in an instant. Her hand whipped out again—this time across the back of Beth's hand—leaving a sting on her palm. "What did I tell you about the bleach?" she hissed.

Beth opened her mouth to apologize, but no words came. She bent to grab a rag, pressing her cheek to the cold tile as she mopped. Each pass of the rag trembled under her mother's gaze. Mary Lee struck her calf with the palm of her hand. Beth gasped, the rag twisting in her grip. "Can't trust you with the simplest task," she muttered, her voice low but lethal. Her hand rose again—Beth flinched, braced herself—but Mary Lee caught herself at the last moment, gripping Beth's hair instead and yanking her head upright.

Tara, perched on a stool at the ledger, froze mid-word. Her pencil hovered over the page. She stared at Beth's reddened wrist, but didn't move.

Beth knelt, one hand bleaching the floor, the other rubbing her scalp, her shoulders tight. Her breath hitched; tears threatened. To cry would be to admit defeat. She worked the rag in slow, steady circles, her knuckles white.

A soft chime at the door made Beth's heart slam. She looked up to see Mrs. Meeks– the schoolteacher at the Colored school– slipping inside. Slender and composed, hair the color of moonlight, skirt pressed, rimless glasses perched on her nose. Every step was measured authority.

Mrs. Meeks set a canvas bag of linens on the counter. Mary Lee wiped her hand on her apron, then tapped Beth's shoulder hard enough to make her knees buckle. Beth righted herself as Mary Lee straightened her own posture and offered a tight, courteous smile to the visitor. "Afternoon, Missus Meeks. You here for the linens?"

Beth swallowed hard, her bruised cheek pressing against her shoulder as she remained on her knees, the damp rag still in her hand. She hadn't spoken a word since the first lash, and now, under Mrs. Meeks's cool gaze, she dared not.

Mrs. Meeks nods, then slides her gaze to the back of the shop, where Beth is still mopping up the spill. She does not speak until she is sure Beth has noticed her attention.

"I see you keeping your girls busy," she says, voice gentle but with an undertow that draws every word toward a hidden agenda.

Mary Lee answers, "Better they know what it means to work, than have the world teach them later."

"True," Mrs. Meeks allows. She inspects the stack of laundered tablecloths Tara brings forward, running her hands over the fabric with a tenderness reserved for rare things. "Your Tara's got a good head for numbers, I can see that. Reminds me of myself, when I was her age."

Beth waits for the comparison to come, but Mrs. Meeks doesn't offer it, at least not aloud. Instead, she addresses Beth directly.

"Would you be so kind as to help me carry these out to my car?"

she asks, as if Beth has a choice.

Beth wipes her hands, sets the bleach-stained rag aside, and moves forward with measured steps. The air up front is easier to breathe, the light softer, the scent of steam and detergent less oppressive than the toxic cloud in the back. She lifts the bundle of linens, surprised at its weight, and follows Mrs. Meeks out the door.

The parking lot is mostly empty, the heat radiating up from the tarmac in lazy waves. Mrs. Meeks unlocks her car, then stands aside to let Beth load the bags onto the back seat. For a moment, neither speaks. The world is reduced to the click of the car door and the distant sound of a lawnmower two streets over.

"You got your mama's strength, child," Mrs. Meeks says finally, watching Beth with a steady, unblinking eye. "Not everyone would call that a blessing, but I do. Means you can take a licking and keep on moving."

Beth does not reply. She is unsure if the words are meant as comfort, or warning, or both.

"Don't let her break you, though," Mrs. Meeks adds, so softly that Beth is unsure if she's heard it at all.

Beth closes the door, and for one breathless second she stands in the late afternoon sun, feeling the weight of the air without the taste of judgment in it. Her shoulders drop. She draws a slow, steady inhale, holds it, and lets it go.

The bell over the laundromat door gave its delicate chime, but it was well past closing, and the shop had gone quiet save for the slow hum of the big washers winding down. Mary Lee, stationed at her habitual post by the counter, greeted the tall man with a look that measured the bulge in his suit pocket before it ever reached the surface.

Wilbur stepped inside, hat in hand, his coat pressed and shoes shined so bright they caught the fluorescents like tiny stars. He looked too substantial for the room, broad-shouldered and calm, his hands clean and knuckles thick from honest work. There was careful dignity in the way he spoke—low and polite, drawl softened by what sounded like years of swallowing pride.

"Evening, Miss Payton," he said, sliding a folded bill across the counter. "I was told I could get a room for an hour or so."

Mary Lee's eyes flicked to the stairs. "Up there," she said, voice clipped. "You'll find what you need."

As Wilbur mounted the stairs, Beth was coming down, arms full of towels. She caught just the edge of his scent—something like cedar and bay rum, nothing perfumed, nothing cheap. Their eyes met halfway. Beth, cheeks flushed from work, hesitated, suddenly aware of the bleach stains on her dress and the lye-roughened skin of her hands. She looked at the thick roll of bills in his palm, the way he tucked it away without flourish.

He paused, offered her a gentle nod. "You working late, miss?"

She blinked, unsure if he was teasing or truly seeing her. "Somebody has to."

Wilbur offered a gentle, knowing smile. "Hard work's honest work. But sometimes the world don't pay fair."

He lingered, his gaze steady and kind. "If you ever want to get outta this place—really get out—come find me by the churchyard after dark. Be glad to walk you home, or anywhere else you might want to go."

"Sure...."She watched him finish his climb, the stairs creaking under his weight. Something about the way he carried himself —no swagger, no drunken leer—made Beth burn with curiosity. Something about his quiet assurance—and the promise tucked in his words—worked under her skin like a secret hope. He could have spent that kind of money anywhere, but he'd brought it here, to this tired building, to her mother's brothel of all places.

At the landing, Tara emerged from behind the ledger, her frame thin and almost delicate in the dim light. She moved with practiced precision, her pale scarf and pressed dress always untouched by the stains that marked Beth's own uniform.

Beth lingered at the landing, listening to the faint click of door latches, the murmur of voices behind thin doors, and wondered what it would be like to have that kind of choice—to simply pay a price, and walk where you pleased.

Beth returns to the laundromat. The light inside is yellower now, the day on its last legs. Mary Lee and Tara are at the counter, heads bent over the ledger, their conversation a hushed duet of numbers and strategy. Beth resumes her place at the utility sink, finishing the task as if nothing has happened.

At five-thirty, Mary Lee rings the bell for closing. The remaining customers pack their things and shuffle out, some nodding in thanks, a few leaving with a sideways glance at the family behind the counter. Tara counts the till, closes out the register, and brings the ledger for a final inspection.

Mary Lee takes the day's earnings and disappears into the office at the back of the shop. When she returns, she doles out the wages, envelope by envelope. Tara's is thick, almost ceremonial. Beth's is thin, the bills inside nearly flat against the paper.

"Thank you, Mama," Tara says, voice sincere.

Beth says nothing. She tucks the envelope into her pocket, careful not to show the crease in her brow.

The sisters walk home together, but not side by side. Tara strides ahead, her steps quick, almost buoyant. Beth lags a few paces behind, eyes fixed on the shifting shadows at her feet. The town is cooler now, the sky streaked with orange and lavender, the day's heat reduced to a memory.

As they pass the church, the bell tolls once, then falls silent. Tara glances back, her face soft in the dusk.

"You coming, Beth?" she asks, not impatient, just wanting to know.

Beth nods, and quickens her pace. They walk the last block together, neither speaking, the space between them as tangible as the road itself.

When they reach home, Tara goes inside first, heading straight for the kitchen. Beth lingers on the porch, letting the evening air dry the last of the bleach from her skin.

From the open window, Mary Lee's voice carries out plans for tomorrow—tasks to complete, rules to follow, expectations to meet. Beth sits on the stoop, legs tucked beneath her skirt, and listens. The knot that had lived between her shoulder blades all day loosens slightly. Not hope exactly, but the absence of hopelessness.

She watches night claim the last purple streaks from the sky. Nothing around her has shifted, but something inside her has—a small, quiet certainty that change is still possible, even for her.

CHAPTER 2

Dawn in the laundromat does not so much arrive as seep in, sly and incremental, a slow dilation of the shadows until every corner stands revealed.

Tara is first at the counter, precise as clockwork. She has her ledger open, spine pressed flat beneath her hand, and she tallies the receipts from the weekend with an exactitude that might have made her the envy of any bank in Little Rock. Her dress, pale blue and clean, clings to the straight line of her back as she writes; her hair is pinned, not a strand out of place, though the work is not yet half an hour begun. Every motion is deliberate. She sits above the rumble and clang of the machines as if she is above even gravity, the world's filth and labor unable to reach her so long as she keeps her wits sharp and her columns sharper.

Beth is in the rear, as always, on her knees with the floor rag in one hand and the bleach in the other, fingers stung raw from the night before. She scrubs at the grout with a fury that is only partly directed at the mildew. Her dress is the same navy as yesterday, its skirt darkened at the knees where the soap has soaked in; the hem frays and leaves threads wherever she drags it. Beth's arms are corded, brown as pecans and rough as sandpaper from years of the same. The only thing soft about her is her eyes, which today are trained not on the floor but, every few seconds, on the clock above the dryers, as if she is counting the hours until she is old enough to leave.

Mary Lee moves between the sisters, a woman-shaped metronome, her presence measured in the click of patent heels against the linoleum and the subtle weather-changes of her face. When she crosses the floor to the counter, her gaze sweeps over Tara's ledger, not searching for error but ready to pounce if one should present itself. When she pivots back to the wash sinks, she leaves a trail of cold air in her wake, and Beth, tracking her with peripheral vision, ducks her head before the blow can land.

"You balancing it in ink or pencil this time?" Mary Lee asks, her tone neither friendly nor hostile, simply unchallengeable.

Tara holds up the page, neat as a pharmacy label. "First draft in pencil, but I'll copy over in pen when I'm done. Yesterday's receipts and carryover from the safe are both here. There's an extra three dollars from the soda machine; I found it stuck behind the coin return."

Mary Lee nods, one slow dip of the head, but the gesture is so slight as to be barely more than a muscle spasm. "Count twice before you write. If the numbers are off, the fault's yours."

"Yes, ma'am," Tara says, her voice calm, almost buoyant. She pencils in a sum, then erases, then rewrites, as if the act of calculation is both a ritual and a test she must daily pass.

At the sinks, Beth can hear every syllable. She wishes she could tune them out, but it is impossible: their voices find her no matter how hard she scrubs. She splashes more bleach on the rag, breathes in the chemical ache, and redoubles her effort, working in tighter, more desperate circles. There is an unspoken contest here, one that is played out every morning, every year of their lives: Tara, the favored, the clever, the paler and more perfect. Beth, the mule, the strongback, the one whose love must be earned a day at a time.

Mary Lee pauses at the midpoint between the two, arms folded, the thin willow switch in her right hand tapping against her skirt. Her eyes narrow at a dull patch on the floor. "What do you call that?" The branch whistles as it cuts air, lands with a snap across Beth's shoulder blades. Beth's body jerks but she doesn't cry out. "I said what do you call that?"

"A streak, ma'am." Beth's voice is flat, practiced. She shifts to shield her face, knowing better than to rub where the welt is already rising.

Tara looks up from the ledger, her pencil frozen mid-calculation. "I can help after I finish the books," she offers, the words barely audible over the hum of machines.

Mary Lee rounds on Tara, the willow branch now pointed like an accusing finger. "You have enough to do."

Tara blinks, stung, but only nods and returns to her numbers. Beth, for her part, does not reply, but the set of her jaw makes clear she would have declined the offer regardless.

The morning swells. First come the widows and day laborers, then a clutch of schoolchildren in uniforms, their socks already sliding down by the time they reach the folding tables. The machines ramp up to a roar, the heat rising in shimmering sheets from their spinning hearts. Tara handles the customers with a bright, efficient patter—"Good morning, how many?" and "That machine's ready for you, ma'am"—never letting her customer service mask slip, even when a man lingers too long at the counter or a woman slides her a tip with fingers lingering against her wrist.

Beth is relegated to the back unless she is summoned. She loads the industrial washers with sheets still damp from the hospital, sorts rags from the fish market by color and degree of foulness, and hauls pails of soapy water until her arms ache and her brain floats free in the caustic clouds. When she surfaces for air, she finds her mother's silhouette always there, waiting, appraising.

At nine sharp, Mary Lee begins the teaching. She stands behind Tara, hands resting lightly on the girl's shoulders, and explains the mysteries of ledger and invoice, how to calculate break-even points and recognize a check that will bounce. Her tone is low but rich, the kind of voice that would be loving if it were not also a warning.

"Never let your guard down with a customer," she says, eyes fixed on the door even as she speaks to Tara. "It's not the ones who holler that you have to worry about. It's the ones who smile, the ones who act like you're just the same as them. They'll take you for a fool and leave you holding the bag."

Tara nods, copying the words into her notebook.

"Memorize the faces that come in, but don't ever memorize their stories. Don't get soft," Mary Lee continues, "soft girls end up behind, or in trouble."

Tara's pencil pauses for just a moment. "Yes, ma'am," she says, but this time there's a tremor in it, so faint you'd need an oscilloscope to catch it.

Beth hears all of this. It is, in its way, a familiar sermon, but each time it lands differently, like a stone thrown at a different angle into the same pond. She wonders if Tara is really listening, or if she is only learning the lines, the way she did for school plays: repeat what's needed, then slough it off when the curtain falls.

By noon, the air is gelatinous with humidity, the ceiling fans rotating in slow penance for their inefficacy. Tara counts the register a third time, then locks it, keys clinking in her palm as she retreats to the back office to tally up. For a brief moment, Beth and Mary Lee are alone in the main room.

"Didn't you finish that drain yet?" Mary Lee says, voice flat but with a rasp that signals danger.

Beth wipes her brow with the back of her wrist, smearing a

crescent of damp onto her forehead. "Almost done. The scrub brush keeps catching in the grate."

Mary Lee steps closer, heels punctuating each syllable. She stoops, snatches the brush from Beth's hand, and demonstrates with two quick, savage strokes that the task is not as impossible as Beth has made it seem. "You got to use your weight," she says, "not just your arms. All this strength in you, but you never know how to use it." She stands, hands Beth the brush, and pivots away, her skirt swishing at knee level.

Beth, cheeks burning, applies herself to the task. She does not look up when Tara returns, or when the lunch rush enters, or even when her knuckles crack and bleed a little onto the tile.

At the counter, Tara rings up a regular and bags his shirts. He smiles at her, leans in just a hair too close, and says, "You always so good at math, or you just practice on me?" Tara returns the smile, but her eyes flick to the side, searching for escape.

Mary Lee interjects, sharp as a cleaver: "My daughter is good at everything she puts her hand to." Her stare freezes the man's joke in his throat. He pays, leaves, the bell above the door jangling like a nervous system.

Tara breathes out, then glances toward Beth, who is watching through a curtain of damp hair. Their eyes meet, just for a heartbeat. Tara's gaze is apologetic; Beth's, electric with something harder to name. Not anger, not envy, but a slow-cooked hurt that could keep for years without spoiling.

Neither sister breaks the silence.

In the lull before the next customer, the only sound is the steady churn of the big washers, and the low, wounded whine of the steam press as it struggles to keep up. Mary Lee stands at the midpoint again, the sun slicing through the glass door behind her and framing her in white. The effect is nearly spectral: for an instant, she could be mistaken for something ancient and pitiless, a monument in a church that no longer holds any god.

She surveys her girls, one at the register, one at the floor, both forged in her image but bent by different hammers. "I want that mop water changed before closing," she announces, already knowing it will be Beth who does it.

"Yes, ma'am," says Beth.

Tara, catching the cue, says, "I'll help her, after I finish with the receipts." But the words have no muscle in them, no real will. She and Beth both know how the day will go.

By midafternoon, the morning's rhythm has collapsed into something closer to a trench warfare: each girl holding her post, neither advancing nor retreating, their mother stalking the perimeter like a general counting casualties. The air is so thick with steam that condensation beads on the inside of the windows, rendering the street outside a wavering watercolor. Inside, the heat is oppressive, but nobody dares remove their cardigan or loosen their scarf, because the appearance of order must be kept, no matter how dire the climate.

Tara closes the ledger, triple-checks the sum, and brings it to Mary Lee for inspection. The three of them stand at the counter, a tribunal of efficiency, as the numbers are reviewed.

"You did good," Mary Lee concedes, after a long inspection. The praise is precious, and Tara basks in it for a brief, unguarded moment.

Then Mary Lee turns to Beth. Her hand flies out, catching Beth across the face with a crack that echoes off the tile. "You missed the corner by the dryer again." Another blow lands on Beth's shoulder, then her back as Mary Lee pushes her against the wall. The beating branch appears from nowhere, whistling through steam-thick air. Beth's uniform darkens in small patches as she slides down the wall. Tara's gaze fixes on a crimson bloom spreading across the back of her sister's blouse.

Beth says nothing, only breathes through her teeth.

The day lumbers on, the light outside draining from platinum to gray. Still, the family persists, as families do, running on the inertia of habit and the faint, always-fading hope that tomorrow will be lighter, that some shift in fortune or mercy will rescue them from the geometry of their labor.

When the last customer leaves, the three of them stand in the center of the room, each in her prescribed space, the air between them thick as soup. Beth's hands are raw and red, Tara's shoulders squared but tired, and Mary Lee—Mary Lee is as she has always been, and perhaps as she always will be: unbending, vigilant, alone.

The girls exchange one last look, Tara's full of apology, Beth's of unspent anger, but neither speaks. The moment hangs in the steam like a confession, unspoken, waiting for the next day to dissolve it.

And outside, the sun has gone, leaving only the blue-white hum of the laundromat's lights to mark their place in the world.

Midafternoon draws a line across the day, dividing the laundromat into two unequal hemispheres: the hush of after-school girls circling each other in packs near the dryers, and the stagnant heat of the front counter where Tara returns to the numbers, their precision a shield against the subtle horror of unfilled hours. The sun has shifted its aim, spotlighting the cash register and bleaching everything it touches into the color of bone.

Beth is in her customary exile, head down in the slop sink. She has mastered the art of scrubbing without appearing to move, her gaze tracing the spider cracks in the basin while her hands work blindly at a rotary of rags. The scent of bleach is so omnipresent she hardly notices it anymore, except when the door opens and a fresh wave of outside air briefly dilutes the tang.

It is in one of these moments—a brief corridor of wind and silence—that a White woman enters. Her shoes are the first thing to announce her: neat, unscuffed, their heels making contact with the rubber mat as if seeking to erase the memory of every step that came before. She wears a wool coat though it's too late in the year for such, and her hair is set in a lacquered swirl that seems designed to resist the environment rather than comply with it. She moves with the bright, performative friendliness of a city councilwoman, nodding at Tara before she even reaches the counter.

"Good afternoon, young lady," she says, voice crisp as celery, and places a muslin bag of linens on the counter with both hands, as if laying a peace offering at the altar.

Tara's posture shifts—shoulders down, chin up—her smile a perfect facsimile of genuine welcome. "Afternoon, ma'am," she replies, ringing the bell under the counter as her mother requires for every walk-in during non-peak hours. She weighs the bag with one hand, bracing herself for the microsecond of physical contact as the woman's knuckles graze hers. There is nothing improper in the touch; still, Tara feels the tremor in it, a split-second calculation of skin color and then the discipline to ignore it.

Mary Lee emerges almost instantly from the back, footsteps deliberate, but with less velocity than the situation warrants. She appraises the scene—a white woman, Tara at the counter, Beth with her head half-submerged in a tub of gray water—and decides on the proper arrangement of face and voice.

"Help you with a drop-off today?" she asks, each word a discrete unit.

The customer turns, produces a smile so wide the creases at her lips threaten to break skin. "I've heard so many good things about this place," she says, eyes flicking from Mary Lee to Tara, then back. "My usual laundress is down with the mumps, and I was told you're the best in town for tablecloths and fine things." She leans into the compliment, each syllable carefully placed, as if she has read somewhere that Black-owned businesses respond best to the currency of praise.

"We do our best," Mary Lee says, polite but flat, and gestures for Tara to open the bag and check the contents.

The moment is a pantomime: Tara unknots the cord, peels the bag open, and inspects the neat stack of snow-white damask, each piece folded with geometric precision. She counts them aloud: "One, two, three, four...six napkins, two runners, and a twelve-foot tablecloth." Each count is a heartbeat, a marker of time passing.

"Impressive," the customer says, watching Tara's hands. "Do you do all this yourself, or do you have help?" She points, as if by accident, at Beth, whose head emerges from the sink just in time to catch the question.

Tara glances back at her mother before replying. "We all help," she says, and Mary Lee nods once, as if to confirm.

The customer's gaze lingers on Beth for a half-beat too long, then slides back to Tara, then to Mary Lee, as if searching for a genealogical answer. She licks her lips, rehearsing the next line. "You must be so proud. It's just wonderful to see your kind running such a respectable place. I'll tell all my friends."

The words hang in the air like smoke. Beth hears them, the phrase "your kind" jangling in her head the way a loose screw will rattle in a machine for days before it does real harm. She lowers her eyes again and pretends not to listen.

Mary Lee's response is almost musical in its timing. "We are Colored folks, ma'am. Not White, if that's what you mean." Her tone is all velvet and no blade, but the correction lands with perfect clarity.

The customer flushes, the color rising from collar to cheekbone in a wave that cannot be disguised. "Oh, I didn't mean—I'm so sorry, I just—" She glances at Tara, then at Beth, then finds no safe place to land her eyes. "I meant it as a compliment. I really did."

"I understand," Mary Lee says, and her smile is so practiced it looks like muscle memory. "We take pride in our work, regardless of what folks expect."

For a moment, nobody moves. Then Tara, whose hands have been motionless on the damask, clears her throat. "Did you want starch with these, or just pressed?"

The customer seizes the lifeline. "Oh, just pressed. My husband can't stand the stiffness. And if you could do the runners with a French fold—?"

"We can do that," Tara replies, writing it down. Her knuckles are white against the pen.

The woman fumbles in her purse, produces two crisp bills, and lays them on the counter. "For the trouble. I'll be back Wednesday, is that alright?"

Mary Lee's eyes don't leave the customer's face. "Wednesday's fine. It'll be ready."

The woman turns, nods a last awkward time, and departs, the bell on the door ringing with a pitch that feels somehow accusatory. The silence that follows is a different species than before—denser, more pressurized. Tara stands rigid at the counter, her hand hovering over the register, while Mary Lee watches the street as if expecting some ghost to materialize in the empty sidewalk.

Beth, who has not moved, allows herself one deep breath before returning to the sink.

Mary Lee breaks the silence first. "You see how they do?" she says, voice lower, aimed at Tara but loud enough for both girls. She softens her gaze, but it's still a scrutiny. "Don't you let them fool you, Tara. They'll clap for you in the store and cross the street when they see you out in the world."

Tara nods, face blank, but her hands tremble just enough for Mary Lee to notice.

"You're too pretty for them to know what to do with," her mother continues, voice pitched as if reading from an etiquette manual and a field guide at the same time. "Don't you ever let a smile trick you. They'll smile right up until the day they can't use you anymore."

Tara doesn't answer. She places the bills in the drawer, writes the customer's name on the manifest, and locks the register. Her motions are less sure now, more rehearsed than natural.

Beth, listening, lets her hands go limp in the sink. The water settles, the bubbles gone. She thinks about the phrase, "your kind," how it can mean everything and nothing in the same breath, how it can be shaped by a smile and yet still slice you up inside.

Mary Lee turns to the back. "You done with that drain?"

"Almost," Beth replies.

"Finish up, then take a break. I need you both fresh for the evening loads."

Beth watches her mother recede into the office, then steals a glance at Tara, who remains at the counter, eyes fixed on the empty place where the customer stood. There is a tremor in Tara's jaw, but she wills it away, closes the ledger, and returns to work.

Beth wonders if this is how it always will be: the world coming at them, one customer at a time, and their only defense the lessons handed down like laundry lists—keep your head down, your hands clean, your story to yourself. She wonders if the White woman will tell her friends about the mistake, or if she will smooth it out in her memory, erase the moment from the record of her day.

Beth changes the mop water, wrings the old one out, and tips the dirty bucket into the drain. The bleach fumes swirl around her, sharp and bitter, but she breathes it in anyway.

When she returns to the main room, Tara is already gone, the counter empty but for the muslin bag and the white damask, folded with care.

Beth lets her fingers rest on the fabric. It is smooth, almost slick, nothing like the callused skin of her own hands.

She finishes her tasks in silence, the lessons of the day settling into her like lye into a cut—slow, corrosive, and impossible to forget.

Closing time in the laundromat always arrives in a fugue state. The machines, stripped of their burdens, drone to an aimless halt; the lights go amber as the sun pivots west, bruising the linoleum in slanted, viscous rectangles. The air is sodden, more chlorine than oxygen, and the only sound now is the feeble song of a single ceiling fan working to keep up appearances.

Beth waits until the last customer has slunk off, the bell on the door signaling her freedom. Tara, face slack from the day's accumulations, stacks the receipts and heads for the office, leaving the counter unguarded. Mary Lee, having corralled the tips and stowed the safe's contents, disappears into the inventory closet for what she calls "the final audit," a ritual that can stretch to half an hour if the numbers aren't to her liking.

Beth slips through the washroom without a word, peeling off her damp sneakers in the harsh glare of the overhead light, then steps into the furnace of the back alley. The bricks behind the laundromat still glow with the sun's last fury; the dumpsters reek of decay and regret. Sweat beads at her hairline. Evening's shadow creeps in, hesitant. She threads left, then right, and halts in churchyard.

Wilbur Parks is already there, leaning against corrugated tin, as if staking claim. He's fifty, a rigid sculpture of muscle and scars— a limp from shrapnel that struck him in the Korean War, burns twisting across his knuckles like highways gone wrong. Rumor says he walked out on his first wife—eleven kids back home— because she "got too smart" with him. But he knows Beth never will—she has already been broken in, broken down.

His grey eyes fix on her, hungry and unreadable. He lusts for her innocence, her freshness, her youth.

"You came," he says quietly, his clipped tone soft around the edges.

Beth wraps her arms around herself, forcing her hands to still. "I said I would."

"You sure about this?"

Her throat tightens. "I can't do it anymore. Every day she finds a new way to shrink me. I'm terrified I'll just—" She stops, dread choking the rest.

He holds her fingers, voice low and steady. "You ain't your mama's property. You're not stuck unless you let her keep you here."

Her gaze fixes on their shoes on cracked asphalt—two battered soldiers. "What if I am?" Her voice cracks.

He waits, silent. Then: "You're not. But if you were, I'd still take you. All I've got is a small house and these two hands—good enough to build a life that won't rot away."

Her chest tightens with a mix of hope and fear. "She'll never forgive me," she whispers.

Wilbur tilts his head, his's stare drilling into her. Then a thin smile. "She'll have to. Or she won't. Doesn't matter. I got you."

Her shoulders slump. "I don't want a wedding. Not now. Just a place where I'm not her disappointment."

He nods, jaw stubbled. "You'll get that. We can leave tonight—my buddy's truck'll roll us past the county line before dawn."

Beth shakes her head, conflict warring in her eyes. "No. If I go, I do it right. Three days. I finish the week, grab my pay, tell her myself."

He lifts her hands to his weathered cheek, fingers lingering. "Three days, ma'am," he says, mock-formal. "You're the boss."

For a moment they stand in the mosquito-thick air, the weight of everything unspoken. Then Wilbur slips back into shadow. "Be safe. And if she hurts you—" He swallows. "You come find me."

"I will," Beth says, though her throat burns.

She waits for his boots to fade, then retraces her steps. Inside the laundromat, the fluorescent glare inspects her like an X-ray. Tara counts change at the counter, jaw set. Mary Lee hides behind the office door's tiny spyhole. Beth hauls the mop bucket to the utility sink, bleach stinging her lungs, her mother's gaze burning her back.

Tara's gone when she returns. Mary Lee stands at the counter, ledger open but eyes on Beth. "Forget something out there?"

"No, ma'am," Beth says, voice steadier than she feels. "Just needed air."

A beat. "Be here early tomorrow. Don't be late."

Beth nods, heart pounding. In the staff room, she closes the door softly, sits on the cot, and presses her hands to her knees. Three days. Promise and fear clash in her chest. She closes her eyes, breathes deep—bleach and hope mingling in her lungs. Outside, dusk swallows the street. Inside, Beth feels more alive than she has in years.

CHAPTER 3

The laundromat buzzed with the familiar sounds of washers and dryers, the air thick with the scent of bleach and damp fabric. Sunlight streamed through the tall windows, illuminating the dust motes that danced lazily in the air. Behind the counter, Mary Lee Payton observed the world through half-closed eyes, her mind calculating profits as her daughters moved through the rows of machines.

At the far end of the laundromat, Wilbur King stood just inside the door, a mix of nervousness and determination coursing through him. He shifted his weight from foot to foot, the sun casting a long shadow across the linoleum floor. Taking a deep breath, he approached Mary Lee, his heart thudding in his chest.

"Mrs. Payton," he began, his voice steady but respectful. Mary Lee looked up, her expression shifting from indifference to curiosity.

"Wilbur," Mary Lee said, arms folded, her voice as cool as bleach water. "What do you want?"

He swallowed, feeling the heat in his cheeks. "I've come to ask your blessing to marry Beth."

Her eyebrows shot up. "You think you can just waltz in here and ask for my daughter's hand? What do you have to offer? You're just a pecan picker."

He met her gaze without flinching. "I don't have a lot, but I work hard." He paused, then added: "To show you I'm serious, I'll pay you monthly installments—for your lost labor here."

Mary Lee's eyes narrowed as she weighed his words. "So you'll give me money every month?" she asked.

"Exactly." Wilbur's voice was steady. "I'll cover every hour you lose, and then some, until I can support both Beth and myself without question."

A slow, calculating smile curved her lips. "Monthly installments, huh? That's more than most young men would promise for a girl like her. I'll consider it."

Wilbur felt hope surge. He bowed his head. "Thank you, Mrs. Payton. I promise I'll prove myself."

She nodded once. "Remember, Beth is my daughter. I won't have her taken for granted."

"I understand," he said.

With a curt wave, Mary Lee turned back to her ledger. Wilbur stepped into the glare of the midday sun, chest tight with promise.

Inside, Beth stood bent over a dryer, her back to the office window. He approached quietly. "Beth."

She straightened, shoulders stiff. "Wilbur! What did she say?"

He took her hands, rough and determined. "She'll think it over. I offered to pay her monthly installments for every hour of work she loses because of us."

Beth's eyes flickered—resignation, then something harder. "How much?"

"Enough," he said, forcing a tight smile.

She dropped her gaze to their clasped hands, the harsh fluorescence casting sharp shadows across their intertwined fingers. Her throat felt tight. "When do we leave?" she whispered, voice trembling between hope and dread. He squeezed her hand, but she sensed his own hesitation, the quick hitch in his breath. Beyond the glass, Mary Lee stood motionless, her calculating eyes weighing the cost of every promise that tied them together.

Beth's lids fluttered open with the rasp of Wilbur's teeth grinding—an unsettling reminder of the tension coiled in their tiny cabin. The soot-blackened ceiling seemed to press down on her. Sliding free of the thin blanket, her heart thudded with each cautious breath. Dressing in the dim light, she moved on autopilot, fingers fumbling at fabric and buttonholes; even the familiar rustle sounded foreign. A cold draft seized her bare feet as she stepped outside. Dawn's pale light offered a grim comfort —another day, another couple of dollars. Inside, she found Wilbur's bag among the rusted tools: salt pork, a stale chunk of cornbread, a half-empty canteen. She slipped two apples into its worn leather strap, sweetness mingling with bitter anticipation.

When she returned, Wilbur sat on the bed's edge, boots laced. A stray sunbeam lit his grin—a sight that should have eased her, but instead deepened her ache. He leaned in and kissed her cheek, a brief peck that felt more like a prod than a caress.

They stepped out together, their strides tentative and out of sync. Fallen nuts and dry leaves crunched underfoot, reminders of the labor awaiting them.

Beth and Wilbur worked as sharecroppers on a sprawling pecan farm, caught in a cycle as old as the red dirt beneath their feet. Each morning, they rose before dawn to tend the groves, their labor exchanged for the promise of a share in the harvest that always seemed to shrink once the landowner's ledger came out. The arrangement left little room for rest or hope—after the farm took its cut for seeds, tools, and rent, and the monthly payments to Mary Lee, there was barely enough left for flour and salt pork. Still, they had no choice but to endure, knowing that missing even a single day's work meant falling further behind in debts that could never truly be repaid.

They bent to their work beneath the indifferent sun. Each drop of sweat was a bitter testament to their shared fate. They toiled side by side, equals in labor if not in love.

She picked with both hands. Thumb and forefinger: twist and pluck, drop, repeat. At first, the pecans parted easily, skins smooth as silk, but by midday the branches bit back, twigs snagging her arms and drawing blood. Beth ignored the sting. She had learned that pain, once past a certain point, was just another kind of weather.

Wilbur was two rows over, his back an arch of muscle and

sweat. He did not pause, did not slow, even when a sharp twig cut open his palm. Beth watched the blood bead and trickle, then disappear as if the pecans themselves were drinking it. She wanted to warn him to take care, but she knew better: he would only go harder, make a show of how little it mattered.

They broke at midday. The sun was a coin, white-hot, stuck at the top of the sky. Beth and Wilbur walked to the edge of the orchard, where a single elm offered something like shade. The tree was dying, gnarled and half-split by lightning, but its shadow was enough to give them the illusion of relief.

They sat with their backs to the trunk, sharing the canteen. The water was warm and tasted faintly of tin, but they drank it anyway, careful to leave some for the walk home. Wilbur peeled the paper off the pork and ate in slow, thoughtful bites, as if chewing were the best part. Beth had no appetite; she nibbled at one of the apples and spat the brown core into the grass. She ran her tongue over her teeth, finding a chip she did not know was there.

Wilbur wiped his mouth with the back of his hand and turned to her. "You hurting?" he asked. She shook her head, then nodded. "Not bad. Just tired." He nodded too, and they sat in silence, listening to the other pickers as they settled in scattered clusters under the same dying elm. A distant boy began to hum a hymn, high and sweet. Beth closed her eyes and let the song fill her, pushing out the ache for a moment. Wilbur picked up a fallen branch and drew patterns in the dirt—circles and slashes that meant nothing but kept his hands moving.

When the barn bell rang—three hard clangs—they stood and

returned to their rows. Beth did not look back at the elm; she knew it would be there tomorrow, and the day after, and the day after that.

The afternoon was worse. The sun seemed to press down harder, as if it resented the sky for holding it up. By two o'clock, Beth's dress was soaked through, her hair a rope of sweat. Her hands were swollen, the skin at her knuckles raw and white. Still, she picked, and picked, and picked, her mind narrowing to the motion and the sound of pecans thudding in her basket.

Wilbur was silent now, breath coming in short, harsh bursts. She knew his back must be killing him—the old injury from Korea —but he would not stop unless forced. He would not give them that satisfaction.

They worked until the sun sank low enough to make the pecans glow gold. The bell rang again, and the orchard emptied, the pickers moving slow, every step a calculus of pain.

At the shed, Beth and Wilbur weighed their baskets. Hers was lighter than she'd hoped. His was twice as heavy, but she saw the way he winced when he lifted it onto the scale. The tallyman recorded the numbers in his book. He did not look at them, only at the page. "Sign here," he said, sliding the ledger across the counter.

Wilbur signed, then handed the pencil to Beth. Her signature was shaky, but she made it legible. The tallyman said, "See you tomorrow," and nothing else.

At home, Beth tended to Wilbur's hands before her own. She cleaned the cuts with the last of the good water, then wrapped them in strips of flour sack. He sat on the bed, eyes closed, not flinching.

"You did good today," she said, tying the cloth tight. He opened his eyes, looked at her as if seeing her for the first time. "You're the strong one," he said. "Always have been." She felt the sting of pride, and something else, something like despair. They ate the rest of the cornbread in silence. Outside, the sun went down, and the sounds of the orchard—crickets, cicadas—drifted in through the cracks.

When it was fully dark, Beth lay down beside Wilbur and felt the tremor in his body. She held him, as much as he would allow, and thought of all the mornings still to come.

A week later, the landowner's buggy rumbled up, the first time in months he'd been by. He wore a stiff collar and carried a ledger heavy with accounts. He stepped down, dust motes swirling, and called them both to the porch. He thumbed through columns of nuts and costs: baskets, crate fees, mule-hire, and rent. For every dollar earned, three were spent.

When he got to Wilbur and Beth, he frowned, then laughed. "Says here you picked two hundred pounds more than last week. You hiding extra hands out there?" "No, sir," Wilbur said. The landowner flipped the page. "Well, it don't matter. After charges, you still come up short." He looked at Beth, then Wilbur. "You want to eat, you best work harder next time." He closed the ledger, counted out a tense stack of bills, and handed it over. Beth saw, even from a distance, there was never enough.

As the buggy rattled off, Beth watched the dust settle behind him. She went inside, counted the money with Wilbur, and they both saw what they already knew: there was never enough. The world was always just a little hungrier than they were.

Tomorrow, there would be more nuts to pick. And the day after, and the day after that. But tonight, there was this small, peculiar moment: the two of them in the dark, refusing to be afraid.

Beth knew before her body did. She felt it in the change of the air, in the way her skin tightened across her ribs, in the small ache behind her knees that had nothing to do with the orchard. At first, she ignored the signs. Women had always worked through worse. But when the world tilted sideways at sunrise and the taste of breakfast curdled in her mouth, she cursed her own hope.

She kept the secret as long as she could, which was not long. The nausea hit hard and early, and she learned to time her morning runs to the ditch so Wilbur could stand watch, leaning casual against the porch rail, eyes on the horizon for anyone who might notice. He was not the type to ask questions. Instead, he walked slower beside her on the way to the orchard, lingered longer at the shed in the evening, and brought home odd little gifts—a button, a bit of ribbon, a pocketful of red beans he bought at the Chinese market down the road. She did not thank him aloud, but the look she gave him was thanks enough.

The work did not lessen. The orchard was even crueler in June; the nuts hung tight on the limbs, their stems sharp as fishhooks. The sun came up angry every day, and the bugs rose with it— gnats and red ants and slow, bloated wasps that clung to her dress and stung just for pleasure. When she could no longer hide her sickness, she let it pass for heatstroke, bent double in the shade, spat twice, and returned to the trees without complaint. Only Wilbur knew the truth, and he held it close, a shared trespass.

They made it to July before the news spread. The midwife from two cabins over, an old woman with wrists like willow branches, knocked at their door one night with a pot of herbs and the certainty that came from a hundred births attended. "You best get ready," she said, not unkind. "You gon' need two sets of hands come autumn."

Beth felt the pride then, the sharp, dangerous pride of someone with a future at stake. She said nothing, just nodded, and began to mark the days on the wall with the stub of a pencil, tiny vertical lines marching up the rough boards like soldiers in an impossible war.

The cabin became a workshop of dreams. Wilbur spent hours after work piecing together a cradle from scavenged pine. The joints didn't fit, and the bottom sagged, but when he showed it to Beth, she ran her fingers over the edges and said, "It's good. He'll be safe in there." She said "he" because they both agreed, without saying so, that it would be a boy.

Beth sewed diapers from flour sacks, tiny shirts from old

pillowcases. She lined the cradle with flowers she found in the feild—soft as a secret. Sometimes, late at night, she pulled the cradle close to her bed and traced the wood's grain, the roughness of it, the way it held her hope without apology.

The rest of life narrowed to routine. Wake, eat, walk, pick, home. The neighbors softened around her, their words less sharp, as if the coming baby had made her an honorary member of some sacred guild. Even the landowner kept farther away, though his bills arrived sooner and heavier than ever, his signature on the bottom of every page reminding them they were always falling short.

The summer crawled, sticky and relentless, until finally, one afternoon, a storm rolled in from the west. The sky went green, then black, and the rain slapped down in sheets, soaking the orchard, turning the clay to soup. Beth felt the first pain then, a sharp twist deep in her belly, followed by another, then another, closer together. She said nothing at first, just pressed a hand to her side and kept moving. But Wilbur saw. He always saw.

He walked her home through the rain, one hand under her arm, the other braced against his ribs, as if willing her strength to transfer through his skin. By the time they reached the porch, the pains were coming hard and regular. Beth sat on the steps and waited for the world to finish breaking.

Wilbur ran for the midwife, who arrived soaked and out of breath, hair plastered to her skull, eyes shining with purpose. She shoed Wilbur from the room, rolled up her sleeves, and began the slow, brutal business of bringing a child into the world.

The labor was a story told in blood and teeth. Beth was not a screamer, but the pain was so wild, so immense, she found herself biting down on a corner of the mattress, straw filling her mouth, the taste of dust and sweat and old sorrow overwhelming. The midwife hummed to herself, an endless, tuneless drone, and between contractions she fed Beth sips of water and wiped her forehead with a rag that smelled faintly of onions.

Outside, the storm raged. The wind rattled the tin, and lightning flashes illuminated the tiny room in bursts, each one showing Beth a new map of her own agony. She thought she might die. She almost welcomed it. But the midwife just hummed louder, and said, "You got this, girl. You got this."

And then, suddenly, the world narrowed to a single, unbearable instant—a tearing, a release, a cry that was both her own and not her own. She was empty, and then she was full.

The midwife caught the infant, held him upside down, slapped his back, and listened for breath. For a moment, there was only silence. Then a squall, sharp and immediate, filled the room, and Beth felt air rush back into her lungs.

She looked up to see the midwife smiling, a rare and radiant thing. "A boy," she said, wiping the child clean with the hem of her own skirt. "Big, too. Strong hands. He's gonna carry more than just pecans, this one."

Beth took the baby—Jacob, she thought—and held him to her

chest. His fingers were tiny, perfect, but already they gripped her thumb with a force that felt ancient, inevitable.

Wilbur stood in the doorway, soaking wet, his shirt stuck to his back, his eyes wide and soft as wet clay. He looked at his wife, his son, and then at the cradle, which had never looked so sturdy.

He did not speak. He didn't need to.

The storm lasted the night, but inside the cabin all was quiet. The midwife cleaned up, burned the bloody rags in the stove, and left without a word.

Beth lay in bed, the baby at her breast, his mouth searching and finding, his fists kneading her side like a kitten. She felt the ache of her body, but also a strange, buoyant peace, as if she had been lifted from the world's hunger and given a brief reprieve.

Wilbur sat on the edge of the bed, one hand on her foot, the other cradling the back of Jacob's head. "He looks like you," he said, voice barely above a whisper. She shook her head. "He looks like both of us. He's got your mouth." Wilbur ran a thumb across Jacob's lips, and the baby yawned, a sound so sweet and whole it nearly undid Beth. She blinked away the tears, not wanting to waste a single second of seeing.

Outside, the orchard was quiet, the earth soaked and broken, the world remade by water. But in the cabin, a new thing had entered—a hope, raw and unguarded, as hungry as anything Beth had ever known.

She remembered the midwife's words: "Strong hands. He's gonna carry more than just pecans." Beth believed it. For the first time, she allowed herself to believe it.

Jacob learned to walk in the mud behind the cabin, his first steps squelched by the black Arkansas clay and the summer's relentless rain. Beth watched him from the orchard's edge, one hand steady on her basket strap, the other free to wave and, when needed, catch him before he could wander to the lane or the well. At a year old, he was all legs and appetite, the world nothing but a continuous surface to be chewed or climbed.

She carried him into the rows on days when neighbors' children were sick or gone. At first, she tied him to her back with a sheet, the way her mother did way back before she built her laundry mat, but soon enough he was too heavy for her and too stubborn for fabric. Wilbur joked that the boy would be bigger than him by spring, but the pride in his voice was so obvious even the landowner heard it, and his monthly ledger grew longer still.

The next pregnancy came too fast for Beth to adjust her hopes or her body. This time there was no hiding it—the sickness was different, all sharp and sudden, and she was tired from the start, tired in her bones, in her teeth, in the very fibers of her hair. The other women nodded when she mentioned it, said it was always worse the second go-round.

The landowner noticed the change immediately. One morning he appeared on the porch while Beth waited for her slip. "You breeding again?" he asked, shadowing half the steps. Beth nodded. He spat into the dirt and said, "You folks multiply like moles. That means more mouths come harvest." He turned away, leaving Beth to take the papers. Wilbur heard about it later from the tallyman, and when he came home that night there was a set to his shoulders that Beth had not seen before.

"You don't have to go back to work so soon this time," he told her, tracing the curve of her belly with his palm. "He can't make you." Beth shook her head. "You know that's not true. We need every penny, Wil." He pulled her close, rested his chin on the top of her head. "He's not gonna break you," he said. "I won't let him." She pressed her face against his chest and listened to the hollow, hopeful sound of his heart.

The summer was a punishment. Every day, the sun ate away at the color of the sky, bleaching it whiter and whiter until Beth felt she was trapped under a bell jar of light and heat and expectation. Her ankles swelled, her hands cramped, her back screamed each time she bent to the row. She left Jacob in the care of the neighbor's oldest girl, but he was always in her mind, a small gravity pulling at her from behind, even when she should have been thinking only of picking.

When Beth started to bleed one morning—a thin, rusty trickle that soaked through her dress before she could hide it—she was more angry than afraid. She stumbled to the ditch and sat in the weeds, rocking back and forth, her hand clamped tight between her legs. She thought, I won't lose this one. She thought of her mother, of the children lost before her, and of the cradle waiting at home. She thought of Jacob's feet on the plank floor. She thought of Wilbur, and of the promise he once made her: he would do anything to keep her safe. The bleeding stopped by noon. She stood, brushed the mud from her dress, and finished her row. She did not tell Wilbur. She did not tell anyone.

On a storm-battered September night, Marcel arrived amid winds so violent neighbors said the whole county would wash away. The rain drummed the tin roof until it was impossible to hear anything else. Lightning split the sky. Beth knew it was time hours before the first contraction. Wilbur sent for the midwife, but the road was gone, the creek over the bridge and the house three feet underwater. Beth braced herself against the wall and waited for the world to finish breaking.

Jacob, wide-eyed and silent, sat in the cradle, legs pulled up to his chin, thumb in his mouth. Wilbur tried to keep him occupied, but the boy would not leave his mother's side, as if some part of him understood.

The labor was different this time: harder, slower, the pain a deep, grinding pressure. Beth screamed once, then clamped her mouth shut, not wanting the landowner to know she could hurt. The cabin leaked from every seam. Water pooled on the floor, turned dirt to soup, dripped through the roof in a hundred tiny waterfalls. Inside, everything narrowed to the arc of the bed, the shape of Wilbur's hand on her shoulder, the slick weight of Jacob pressing against her leg.

When the baby finally came, it was quick, a burst of wet and blood, and then silence, long enough for Beth to think she had lost him. She reached down, found the slippery body, and held it close, rubbing the back in frantic circles the way the midwife taught her. The baby coughed, then cried—the sound thin, but alive. She lifted him up, showed him to Wilbur, and Wilbur laughed, a choked, desperate laugh that turned to sobs before he could stop it.

"Marcel," Beth said, name blooming in her mind like a weed. The baby opened his mouth as if ready to speak it back.

They cleaned Marcel as best they could with the water they had. Beth wrapped him in the last clean shirt, then tucked him into the cradle beside Jacob, who stared at his new brother with something like awe.

Wilbur sat on the bed, head in his hands, body shaking. Beth sat beside him, leaned her shoulder against his, and they watched the boys together, four hearts beating against the dark.

When dawn broke, the landowner's buggy waited at the fence as always—late, silent, ledger in hand. He never congratulated, only tallied: two children added to the account. The pages filled, debts grew. He slid the papers across the porch rail without a word, then climbed in and drove off, dust swirling behind him.

Beth stood in the doorway, Marcel and Jacob in her arms, and watched him go. The orchard lay beyond, rows and rows of brown heads nodding in the morning breeze. The world was still demanding, still hungry. But in her arms, the two boys slept, small and perfect and, for one brief hour, gloriously safe.

Tomorrow, there would be more nuts to pick. And the day after, and the day after that. But tonight, they were enough. Four bodies in a space barely big enough for one. Four hearts, beating quietly against the dark.

CHAPTER 4

The world begins not with a bang but with the hush that comes before it, a syrupy prelude of silence. The cabin sits crouched among the pecan trees, its outline barely distinct from the shroud of morning fog, a crooked tooth in the jaw of Miller County. Before light even dreams of itself, Wilbur wakes.

He is practiced at this, the art of not waking anyone else. His body, once a lurching collection of parts, has learned stealth by necessity. He slips his legs from beneath the quilt, the movement so slow that the air itself barely ripples. The mattress sags but does not betray him with sound. He stands, feeling the ache of old bruises in his knees, and pads to the corner where the floorboards are uneven.

He kneels, hands curling around the cold wood. His fingers are thick and chewed by years of work, nails blunted and ridged, skin inlaid with the black memory of dirt and oil. He finds the familiar loose slat, teases it up with the tip of one finger, and removes the Bible from beneath. It is not a fine Bible, not even a whole one. Its leather is cracked, the corners gnawed, the onion-skin pages splaying like the feathers of a dying bird. But Wilbur holds it with reverence, as if it is the only proof in this world that he is worth more than the fields.

He sits by the hearth—the cold coals little more than ghosts now—and opens to the Psalms. His lips move, but no sound comes. The verses are a chant, a kind of thinking more than speaking. He does not pray for miracles. He does not pray for money or mercy or an easier boss. He prays that he will not let his children down. He prays for the strength to keep his rage inside his chest, where it belongs, and not let it spill over onto Beth or the kids or the brittle old man at the supply store who calls him "boy" with every receipt.

Behind him, the room is an arrangement of bodies. The children sleep not in rows, but in a heap: three at the foot of the bed, one splayed starfish-style across the middle, the baby curled into the curve of Beth's spine. Time has brought with it three new souls– Isaiah, Angelique and Alphonse. The quilt they share is the same one from their first winter together, now a patchwork of memory, each stain a testament to a spilled broth or a fever night or a long, frantic birth.

Beth does not snore, but even in sleep her breathing is a labor. She is beautiful in the way of women who have survived more than a man expected: her face sharp with hunger, hair braided back so tightly it sculpts her skull. Her hands, even in sleep, are in fists.

Wilbur reads a page, then another, letting the words collect in his mind like silt in a creekbed. He does not mark his place; he knows it by the feel of the paper, the torn edge that lines up with his thumb when he is ready to begin again.

The first child to wake is Alphonse. He does not move, but his eyes open, clear and black as ink. He watches Wilbur for a moment, then, sensing no danger, nestles deeper into the tangle of siblings and pulls the quilt up over his head. The next is Angelique, who sits bolt upright and stares at the ceiling with the judgmental air of a magistrate before declaring, in a loud whisper, "Mama, I gotta pee."

Beth is awake before the sentence finishes. She sits up, her braids stuck to the side of her cheek, and scans the room for threats before registering the hour. "Go on, then, but don't slam the door." Angelique scurries outside, bare feet slapping the boards, and Wilbur smiles at the echo—so like Beth herself, always urgent, always moving toward the necessary.

The rest of the family wakes in a slow, uneven cascade. The baby fusses, then settles; Alphonse emboldened, sits up and stares at the fireplace as if daring it to spark. Marcel is last, refusing to open his eyes even as he rolls into the empty space where Wilbur had lain. Beth's gaze finds Wilbur, and he nods, before putting the Bible back beneath the floor.

The kitchen is Beth's territory. She moves through it with the efficiency of a quartermaster, measuring portions in the palm of her hand, weighing every decision for cost and consequence. The breakfast today is mush: a gruel of cornmeal and water, salted by the memory of lard but absent the lard itself. She dishes it out with a spoon so dented the children call it "the grinner." There is no sugar, but Beth has learned to drizzle a single drop of honey across the top of each bowl, just enough to fool the children's tongues into thinking the day has started sweet.

The table is small, so the children eat in relays, two perched on the bench, one standing with her bowl held up to her chin. Beth eats nothing until the rest are done, scraping the last of the mush from the pot with the side of her thumb. Wilbur drinks coffee—strong, black, and burned—while reading a page from the Farmers' Almanac that he has already memorized.

Outside, the sun is starting its climb, orange at the edges but still low enough to make the world seem half-finished. Beth's eyes find the window again and again, not out of hope, but out of habit. The pecan fields on the far side of the yard are damp with dew, the rows already marked by the tracks of yesterday's labor. Beyond the fields is a line of trees, and beyond that, only what Wilbur calls "more trouble."

It is only as Beth wipes down the table with a rag made from an old shirt sleeve that Wilbur speaks of the church meeting. He does it casual, folding the words into the end of a sentence about chores. "your brother in law, Craig, says there's talk of a gathering tonight. Maybe a few folks at the church basement, after dark. Reverend Michaels, too."

Beth's hands still. For a second, she does not move, the rag held tight in her fist. Then she resumes, slower now, her face unreadable. "You going?" she asks.

Wilbur shrugs. "I reckon. There has been talks fo a sit in. Maybe more."

Beth glances at the window again, then at the children, who are now wrestling in the dirt near the step. "You be careful," she says, but her voice is thin, the concern in it stretched over too many years to hold real shape.

Wilbur does not promise. He knows promises are cheap, and sometimes worse than nothing. Instead, he stands, tucks the shirt he will wear to the orchards into the waistband of his pants, and places a hand on Beth's shoulder as he passes. She does not flinch, but her whole body tenses beneath his touch, a wire strung too tight.

He leaves the cabin with the Bible still hidden, the world outside brightening by the second. The air smells of mud and woodsmoke and the dank, fishy musk of the river. He walks with his head high, but his jaw set tight.

Inside, Beth gathers the children to the table, not for breakfast but for the morning recitation. She teaches them numbers, letters, and the Lord's Prayer, in that order. Her voice is clear, no nonsense, each word landing like a stone on water. When she looks out the window, she sees Wilbur's back growing smaller, the sun glancing off his scalp in a tiny, perfect flare.

She feels the heaviness in her own chest, a weight she cannot name. The day has begun, and there is no turning back.

At night, the church is a different creature. The wooden siding, battered and bleached by years of sun, takes on a blue-black sheen in the absence of daylight. The windows, patched with translucent plastic, throw weak silhouettes onto the dirt outside. If you crouch behind the chimney—like Wilbur does, hands in pockets, collar up against the cold—you can watch the lamp flicker in the basement and count every body that slips in from the shadows. Twelve tonight, not including the preacher. All of them men, though two bring sons (old enough to pass for grown).

Inside, it smells of floor wax and must, but mostly of sweat. The basement is low-ceilinged and damp; the walls sweat even in winter. A single kerosene lamp, perched on a stack of Bibles, casts shadows sharp enough to cut bread. The men sit around a folding table, their work coats steaming where the night air meets the leftover heat of day.

Wilbur takes his place at the end of the table, where the lamplight barely reaches. He puts his hands on the hymnal. The air is thick enough to drink.

Reverend Michaels starts with prayer, as always, but it's a fast one: nothing fancy, just the basics, asking the Lord to keep them safe and give them courage. He keeps his eyes open while he speaks, scanning the faces at the table as if the Devil is liable to show up in a suit. When he's done, he taps the table with a finger.

"We got news out of Greensboro today," the Reverend says, his voice low, each word dipped in gravity. "Four students sat a lunch counter all afternoon, didn't move. Not once. They're Colored, too. Just sat, and let the police carry them out." He smiles, just barely, as if tasting a forbidden thing. "Makes you wonder what we're capable of, don't it?"

The table hums with half-voiced agreement. Old Man Rucker, who runs the filling station, says, "They gonna get themselves killed." His eyes never leave the lamp. "You try that here, Sheriff would have you strung up before the register rang a second time."

"Maybe so," Reverend says, "but sometimes you got to put yourself on the line. Can't keep waiting for somebody else to carry your water."

Wilbur listens, keeps quiet, lets the words pass over him. He's not the oldest here, but he's got more miles than most, and he knows when it's time to keep your powder dry. He studies the lamp instead, the blue of the flame licking at the glass, and thinks about all the things a fire can do—warm a house, light a path, or burn it all down.

A boy at the far end passes a stack of leaflets down the table. Wilbur takes one, unfolds it slow. On the outside, a picture of a ballot box; inside, three steps for registering to vote. Simple, almost childish, but the print is careful. He tucks it into his sleeve, where it joins three others he has yet to hand out.

"We get caught with these," Rucker mutters, "ain't nobody coming for us."

"You scared?" asks Jackson, a younger man, sinewy and wound tight as a watch spring.

Rucker bristles. "Not scared, just smart. I seen what they do to smart men in this county."

Michaels interjects, "Smart don't mean nothing if you don't use it."

The room stills. The lamp hisses, glass sweating in the heat. Wilbur finds the newspaper clipping in the hymnal and reads it again, even though he has memorized every word: "Montgomery bus boycott enters tenth month. Leaders vow to continue. Police double patrols, but city stands firm." He wonders what it would be like to live in a city that stands firm, what it would be like to believe in the certainty of anything.

"Folks in Texarkana say they'll go down to register to vote," Michaels continues. "I told the man from the Tribune, we'd be right behind them. But that means nothing unless we got people willing to step forward." He lets the words hang, looks straight at Wilbur. "Men willing to put their names on the line."

Wilbur holds the gaze. He can feel the eyes of every man at the table, the weight of all their stories, all the times they've had to step aside, nod and smile, make themselves smaller. He thinks of Beth at the window, the kids at the table, the raw bone of hunger that gnaws even in good years. He clears his throat.

"I'll do it," he says, voice low but steady. "Ain't nothing for me on the outside of this, anyway. My children deserve better than picking nuts and going through back doors."

There's a silence, not awkward, but reverent, as if someone has just said a prayer worth believing. Michaels nods, then claps his hands together, once.

"Alright, then. First step is Sunday, after service. We'll walk the line. Just walk, nothing more. Keep our heads high, stay in a row. They want us to break, we don't break."

"Walk where?" asks the boy, voice cracking on the second word.

"To the courthouse," Michaels says. "To register. First group goes in, and when they get sent home, next group goes. We don't stop until every name's on the books or they run out of paper."

Rucker shakes his head, but it's not a no, just the shake of a man who can already see the trouble coming.

"You want me to bring Jacob?" Wilbur asks, voice so soft he's not sure anyone hears.

Michaels answers: "If you trust him to hold his ground."

"I do," Wilbur says. "He's steadier than me some days."

The talk turns to logistics—how to dress, when to meet, which men are in charge of watching the alley for police. Someone mentions food, and they all laugh a little, the tension breaking for a heartbeat. Even in the dark, even in the face of what's coming, they are hungry for life.

Then, suddenly, the room goes still. A siren, distant at first, then nearer, cuts through the night. Michaels stands, snuffs the lamp, and in one motion the table is cleared, pamphlets stuffed into jackets, voices dropped to whispers.

"Split up," he hisses. "If they come down here, we're just singing, you hear?"

The men move fast, chairs scraping, coats pulled tight. The old man and the boy head for the side door, the others out the back. Wilbur and two more stay behind, hymnal open, heads bowed, as if they have been at prayer all night.

The siren fades, turning down the street. No one breathes until it's gone.

Then, in the dark, Michaels starts a hymn, voice low and raw: "Oh freedom, oh freedom, oh freedom over me." Wilbur joins in, his baritone filling the corners of the room. The walls catch the sound and send it back, until the basement feels too small for the song inside it.

When the hymn ends, there is nothing left but the scrape of boots on cement, the shuffle of men climbing stairs one at a time. Wilbur is last to leave. He closes the door behind him, steps into the icy blue of the night, and walks home with the ballot guide pressed flat against his chest, his heart hammering beneath it.

He knows what is waiting for him at home: the children, their hungry dreams; Beth, awake and watching; the fields, endless and ready. He walks anyway, each step a small defiance, each breath a claim on the future.

On the way home, Wilbur walked with the slow, deliberate gait of a man already shadowed by tomorrow. Night had settled thick over the county road—a velvet burden pierced here and there by the brief blink of a porch light, the glimmer of a transistor radio through a neighbor's cracked window. Wilbur kept his hands in his pockets, the ballot leaflet warming against his chest like a hidden vow. Every step, he rehearsed the conversation he would not have with Beth: what he'd raise, what he'd keep close, how his own hope could be counted on not to embarrass itself.

He skirted the muddy lane, boots sticky with last week's rain, letting his mind drift back to the words in the hymn. Oh freedom, oh freedom. The gospel had never meant floating away; for men like him, freedom was heavy. It pressed down, weighted every choice, made the world ache with the knowledge that tonight's silence would break as soon as daylight returned and someone came calling.

Down at the cabin, no lamp burned in the window, but he felt Beth waiting anyway. Her gaze worked like a pulley, drawing him up the steps with a promise sharp enough to cut. He paused on the stoop, brushing grit from his palms, and let the hush wrap around him. Inside, the children were quiet save for the sough of even breath and the stray whimper kicked loose by a dream. He toed off his boots, careful not to scrape the boards, and slipped into the room by the gentle silver of moonlight.

Beth sat at the table, eyes fixed on the chipped cup in her hands. She'd wrapped a scarf over her hair; she wore her guardedness like armor. When Wilbur stepped in, she didn't speak, but he could see the tension in her jaw, the way her tongue pressed against the front of her teeth.

He dropped into the other chair. "We finished before midnight," he said, the lie easy but pointless. "Reverend prayed over us and sent us home. Nothing you'd call dangerous."

Beth grunted, unconvinced. "Heard sirens," she said. "Thought maybe…" The thought trailed off, but the worry hung in the air, bright as static.

Wilbur shook his head. "Nobody came for us. Just a scare." He wanted to add detail—a joke, maybe, about Old Man Rucker and his jumpy hands—but his own nerves were worn too thin for stories.

For a time, neither spoke. He watched her thumb circle the rim of the cup. She stared at the knot in the table's grain, as if waiting for the wood to prophesy. From the bed, the children's bundle rose and fell in sleep.

Finally she asked, "You bringing Jacob on Sunday?" Her words sounded almost like accusation.

Wilbur studied the boy, moon-pale in the morning light, shoulders squared beside his brothers. "Wouldn't trust myself to stand still if it got ugly," he said. "But him…I believe he could."

Beth nodded slowly. "He'd hold himself proud. He's seen enough to know where to put his feet."

Wilbur worked his jaw, rolling the next thought before letting it drop.

The sun climbed toward its zenith, casting a bright promise over the town, yet Wilbur felt a chill of uncertainty. He stood before the county registrar's office, the statute brick façade looming above them. His palms were slick against his trousers. Around him, a line was forming: farmers in dusty hats, church deacons in their Sunday best, young men fresh from work—all waiting their turn. Whispers rippled through the crowd like a breeze stirring dry leaves.

Jacob shifted at his side, his youthful energy taut. "You sure about this, Daddy?" he asked, voice tight with hope and fear.

Wilbur laid a firm hand on his son's shoulder. "We're doing this for a better future, son. For you and your siblings." The weight of responsibility settled on his shoulders like an old coat, yet he squared his back. This was their moment.

Near the front of the line, Reverend Michaels stood tall beneath the courthouse portico, his presence both solemn and sure. He caught Wilbur's eye and offered a small nod.

When it was their turn, the Reverend raised his voice so all could hear. "Remember, we are not merely filling out papers. We are claiming our place in this democracy. Our children will know that we did not wait for equality—we stood and demanded it."

A low murmur of agreement rolled through the line. Wilbur glanced down at Jacob, who stared at the registration window with wide eyes.

"Stay close, son," Wilbur said, squeezing his hand. "Walk in proud. We're not here to beg; we're here to assert our rights."

He stepped forward, Jacob at his heels, and approached the glass partition. A clerk peered at them through the small opening, pen poised.

Wilbur cleared his throat. "I'd like to register to vote."

The clerk's expression tightened. She leaned back in her chair. "Do you have proof of residence?" she asked, voice flat.

Wilbur produced a faded utility bill. Jacob watched as his father's fingers trembled over the envelope.

The clerk flipped pages in a ledger. "Your name's spelled... unusual," she said, scanning the form. "You understand the literacy test?"

Jacob's gaze flicked between his father and the clerk. Wilbur swallowed. "I do," he said firmly.

She handed him a pen. Wilbur filled in the blanks, his signature crisp. Around him, the line grew still, the only sound the scratch of his pen on paper.

When he finished, the clerk slid the form back. "You're registered," she said, though her tone suggested she would have preferred otherwise.

A murmur of encouragement rose from the line—soft but steady. Reverend Michaels clapped Wilbur on the shoulder. Jacob let out a breath he'd been holding, eyes shining.

The clerk called the next name. Wilbur stepped back, Jacob at his side, pride blooming in his chest.

They lingered on the courthouse steps until the line moved on. Wilbur looked at his son. "You did good," he said quietly.

Jacob grinned. "We did good."

Together, they turned away, knowing that today they had claimed not just a piece of paper, but a piece of their future.

The laundromat is alive before the sun is up, before the streets even decide which way the wind will blow. In the back room, Mary Lee sits at a folding table, counting quarters with a rhythm so precise it could run a train on time. Her thumb presses each coin to the surface, one after another, the silver clicking out a staccato over the deep, constant thrum of the washing machines in the next room. The air is hot, sticky with steam and the chemical bite of lye; the only relief is the rotary fan nailed to the far wall, its blades spinning so fast the world outside might as well not exist.

On the desk, a ledger lies open, each page dense with columns: utilities, soap, wages for the girls who mind the front counter after school. Next to it, the day's paper, folded to the story of a riot at Central High. The picture shows a mob outside the school, their mouths open, fists in the air. Mary Lee reads the article twice, then presses it flat, as if the weight of her hand can change the story by pure force.

She has always liked the laundromat at dawn. It is the one place in town she can see the future—hers, her family's—stretched out in neat, predictable increments. Machines wear down, belts snap, hoses clog. But everything can be repaired or replaced, so long as the quarters keep coming.

It is nearly six when the bell above the door tinkles, and Beth enters with her brood in tow. Five children, shades of mohagony and pine, all with the same wide, wary eyes. Beth is first through the door, her hair caught up in a rag, her shoulders squared against the day. The baby rides her hip like a barnacle, eyes fixed on the ceiling tiles as if memorizing a secret map.

Mary Lee watches from her post, noting the drag in Beth's step, the way her dress sags at the hips, how her hands tremble just a little as she shifts the baby from one side to the other. She says nothing about the deepening bags under Beth's eyes. Instead, she greets the oldest child present– Marcel– with a nod, and tells him to start with the mop in the front lobby.

"You keep at those floors until I say stop," she instructs. The boy doesn't flinch, just grabs the bucket and gets to work, shoulders already hunched in the way of grown men.

The other children fan out, each claiming a corner of the laundromat, picking up bits of lint and stray wrappers, collecting bottle caps and odd socks into a wire basket. Their movements are practiced, efficient, not a wasted gesture between them. Even the youngest knows to stay clear of the hot dryer vents and the angry old women who come in first thing with bags of hospital sheets.

Beth wipes down the folding tables, moving slow, as if each swipe costs her a little more than she can spare. Mary Lee waits until she is in earshot, then says, "You look tired."

Beth shrugs. "Marcel was up all night with fever. Wilbur took him out back, tried to walk him calm, but nothing worked."

Mary Lee grunts, then slides a roll of dimes across the table. "Pay yourself from this. The girls at the counter called off, again."

Beth pockets the dimes without thanks. She cleans the next table, then the next, her face a blank.

Mary Lee studies her daughter, the way her eyes flicker to the window every few minutes, as if she's waiting for someone to appear on the stoop. She follows Beth's gaze, sees only the empty parking lot, the sun just beginning to gild the curb. "Wilbur at the church again?" she asks.

Beth nods, not looking up. "Meeting last night. He didn't say what for."

"They ever ask you to help?" Mary Lee asks.

Beth's hand pauses on the cloth, then resumes. "No. I reckon they don't want women at those meetings."

Mary Lee makes a noise in her throat, halfway between a laugh and a cough. She wants to say: Men don't know what to do with a woman who won't be quiet. She wants to say: You're better off without them. But she doesn't, because she knows words have weight, and once dropped, they are impossible to sweep up.

The washing machines drone on, the quarters rattling in their trays. For a time, the only sound is the music of labor: the mop bucket sloshing, the coin sorter's mechanical song, the click of

Beth's rag snapping out a wrinkle.

Then Mary Lee says, "There's jobs in San Francisco. At the car plant. The in-laws have been looking into it."

Ever since Tara married Craig, Mary Lee couldn't stop talking about him and his family's great plans.

Mary Lee leans in."Craig wants better for Tara. Craig's cousin wrote me last week—said they're hiring Colored men by the dozen, maybe more."

Beth stops, cloth in midair, and turns her head, slow. Her eyes are not blank now, but wary, as if she's heard a trap instead of an offer. "We got work here," she says.

Mary Lee shakes her head. "Work, yes. Money, no. The orchards don't pay enough for a man to feed seven mouths, not unless he's on the boss's good side, and Wilbur is never going to be on the boss's good side."

Beth wipes the table harder. "What's in San Francisco for people like us?"

Mary Lee snaps the ledger shut. "Money, for starters. A way out. You want to raise your children in a place where you can't even walk the street without looking over your shoulder?"

Beth doesn't answer, but Mary Lee knows she has scored a hit. She presses on: "You think it'll be better when the kids are grown? You want them breaking their backs for pennies, or worse, getting in trouble for standing up to the wrong man?" She slides the newspaper closer to Beth, taps the front page. "This is what happens when you wait for things to change here."

Beth stares at the photo, her jaw working. The children have finished their chores and now cluster by the door, watching the two women, antennae up for trouble.

Mary Lee leans forward, voice soft. "Craig's family is sending for us. They want to know if we'll take the tickets."

Beth closes her eyes for a long moment, then opens them again, gaze fixed on a patch of sunlight creeping up the wall. "Wilbur won't want to leave," she says, but it is more question than statement.

Mary Lee shrugs. "Wilbur will do what you tell him, if you tell him right."

Beth shakes her head, but the fight is gone from her. She gathers the children, lines them up by the door, and tells Isaiah to carry the baby. Then she looks back at her mother, face set.

"If you think it's right, I'll ask him," she says.

Mary Lee nods, not trusting herself to say more. She watches as Beth shepherds the children out into the blinding morning, their shadows long and thin on the pavement.

The house is quiet when Beth returns, the children sprawled across the floor, asleep before dinner. The kitchen smells of boiled beans and wood smoke; the window over the sink glows blue, then purple, as the day folds itself away.

Beth stood at the kitchen sink, hands plunged into lukewarm dishwater, staring through the wavering pane at the last bruised streaks of sunset. Evening came over the house like a hush: the small, near-silent shifting of children in sleep, a faint gurgle from the baby where Isaiah had propped him on a pallet by the stove, the click of cooled metal as beans dried to paste at the bottom of the pot. The table was wiped, the floor swept, and for the first time all day, her own shadow had room to stretch.

She could feel in her chest the echo of Mary Lee's words, hard as stones settled in a bucket. San Francisco. The phrase sounded impossible, foreign, like a name from a dream or a movie flicker she'd caught once in the foyer of the colored cinema in town. She thought of Tara, always brighter, always chosen, whisked off to something better. She had told her mother she'd ask Wilbur. But now, standing at the sink, dishes done, she could not find the words to begin.

Wilbur returned home late from the church. Beth herd him on the walk before she saw him, the drag of boots through pocked dirt, the careful way he set the latch so it wouldn't wake the children. He came in with the chill on his coat and the scent of sweat and woodsmoke. He didn't look at her at first, just turned to check the hallway, saw that the kids were down for the count, and only then came to stand beside her at the sink.

He was quiet, as he always was after those meetings. She wiped her hands, offered him the last coffee in the pot. He took it, still not meeting her eyes. The silence between them felt thicker than it had in years.

She waited until he'd set his mug down. "Mama says Craig's found work at the car plant out west. In California." Her own voice sounded strange, as if someone else had moved her mouth.

Wilbur nodded once, slow. "He mention what they're paying?"

She shook her head. "Just said it's steady work. Said they're hiring Colored men on the lines."

He leaned against the counter, thumb rubbing at a raw spot on his knuckle. "You thinking we should go?"

Beth looked down at the gray, ridged skin at the back of her own hands. She saw the cracks where the bleach and lye had worked in over the years, and the ghost of her mother's old switch across her knuckles. "I don't see much left here for the children. Not unless we want them working like this, or worse." Her voice dropped. "Marcel's cough won't quit. Winters keep getting longer."

Wilbur listened, gaze drifting toward the window where dusk bled its final colors across the glass. He didn't speak for a long time, and she wondered if he would at all.

Finally: "I got roots here." He said it so softly she barely caught it. "All I know is this ground. The church. Men at the meetings, they look up to me." He looks at the floor. "I never thought I'd leave this place." His voice was thick, almost hoarse. "Never thought I'd be the kind of man to run."

"We won't be running," Beth said, a little louder than she meant.

Wilbur sat at the table, and pulls a map of the United States out of his Bible. The voter's registration pamphlet from the meeting spills out as well— two paths towards a better tomorrow, spread before him. He uncrumples the map. His finger traces a line from Texarkana westward, each town along the way a fresh question mark. He looks up when Beth enters, eyes tired but bright.

"We can try. If it's no good, we come back."

Beth smiles, just a little. "We won't come back."

Wilbur smiles, too, the smallest upturn of lips. He folds the map, stands, and pulls Beth close. They stand like that for a long time, the sounds of the town creeping in through the walls: a train whistle, a dog barking, the distant hum of tires on wet pavement.

For a moment, it is enough. The world outside is vast and dangerous, but here, in this room, they are together, and the future is as wide as the space between stars.

CHAPTER 5

The morning of departure is more ceremony than escape. The stars still hold their posts over Texarkana, pale and anxious, as Mary Lee Payton wipes her hands one last time on the ragged apron she refuses to leave behind. The bleach and starch have worked themselves into her skin so thoroughly that when she presses her palms together, they rasp. She stands at the threshold of the shuttered laundromat, ledger pressed flat under one arm, the other raised to orchestrate the loading of the last battered suitcase.

Her family assembles in the slow, haphazard rhythm of the truly exhausted. Craig arrives first, cradling the one good radio like a newborn. He checks the bus tickets against the timetable for the seventh time, lips moving silently as if the arithmetic might suddenly rewrite itself. Beth and Wilbur herd Jacob and Marcel, the boys still half-dressed and blinking against the night, their limbs moving as if through syrup or a dream. The younger children would accompany them in California once they were settled.

"Get your shoes on proper," Mary Lee snaps. "And mind you don't lose the gloves, neither. You know how your hands go."

The bus is not yellow, nor is it new. Its skin is sun-peeled to a sad approximation of white, and along the sides someone has spray-painted a stuttering line of blue stars, as if patriotism might keep the engine from dying in the first hundred miles. The driver —a White man with a sunburned scalp and eyes like refrigerator bulbs—waits with the engine running, fingers drumming on the steering wheel. When he sees the Paytons and Kings, he jerks his chin in a motion so brief it might be a tic. The door creaks open on a hiss of diesel and surrender.

Wilbur lifts Marcel onto the first step. He turns to reach for Jacob, but the elder boy is already inside, face pressed to the fogged glass, watching for a sign that the world outside is worth returning to.

"Let the boys sit together up front," Mary Lee commands, climbing the stairs. "I'll be just behind."

Craig boards last, lugging a duffel whose seams groan with every step. He deposits it in the aisle, then wedges himself into a seat behind the boys, where he can watch the whole family in a single sweep.

The bus smells of rubber, old food, and the particular flavor of men who sweat through uniforms but never break a real sweat at their jobs. The heater is set too high, and every surface exudes a sticky, suspicious dampness. The children do not complain. They have never been on a bus before, and it is enough to sit, to bounce in the molded seats, to feel the whole world jolt as the driver slams the doors and releases the brake.

The city sags behind them with a slow, cataclysmic indifference. The first mile is nothing but the familiar pecan groves that they have grown to both love and hate. The second mile brings cotton fields, and with them the memory of the lives left behind: the rows of stunted cotton, the splintered telephone poles marching into infinity, the modest houses crouched against the wind.

Mary Lee watches the passing landscape with a stillness that is almost violence. Her gaze is unblinking, her hands folded so tightly in her lap that the knuckles glow white. At each crossroads she marks their progress with a silent inventory: one mile closer, one burden lighter, one debt less to drag behind them. She does not look at the children, or at Wilbur, or at Craig.

Her vision is fixed on the horizon, the future strung taut before her like a bedsheet on a line.

Behind her, the boys have invented a game: count the cows, count the trains, count the men in hats. Jacob cheats, but only a little, and Marcel howls each time he is caught, the sound equal parts delight and outrage. Their mother, Beth, sits across the aisle, hands curled in her lap, eyes half-closed as if she is practicing for the arrival of sleep, or death, or whatever comes first. When she catches Mary Lee's glance, she offers a flicker of a smile, a confession of fatigue more than kinship.

Wilbur occupies the seat directly across from Mary Lee, his body angled to face the aisle. He has dressed in his best shirt, a blue one with a fraying collar, and his shoes are polished to a hard, improbable shine. He carries no book, but his lips move anyway, murmuring scripture or maybe just the remembered pattern of a long-ago prayer.

Craig sits behind the boys but does not interact. He leans his head against the cold window, eyes half-shuttered, the thumb of his left hand tracing slow, deliberate circles on the metal frame. Every few miles, he exhales a sigh so soft it barely moves the air.

As the sun claws its way up, the inside of the bus becomes a theater of shifting light and shadow. Every head is haloed, every gesture made larger and stranger by the play of early sun through the grimy glass. The landscape, meanwhile, flattens out into a geography of sameness: one field, one road, one clump of trees repeated to the vanishing point. The only variation is in the telephone lines, which sag deeper and lean further the farther west they travel.

The driver does not speak except to issue periodic reminders —"Rest stop in twenty," "Hold your trash," "No standing"—each one delivered in a tone so disinterested it seems a marvel that he bothers to say anything at all. When the bus finally does pull over, it is at a filling station whose signage has been half-erased by sun and wind, the faded shell of a brand no one remembers. Mary Lee is the first off, guiding her flock to the bathroom line.

Inside, the restroom is its own kind of battlefield: too few stalls, too many bodies, a floor slick with the legacy of a hundred careless strangers. The boys are sent in together, warned to keep hands clean and eyes forward. Mary Lee waits outside, arms crossed, ignoring the looks from the White women who smoke near the door.

Beth stands to the side, her back to the wind, hair unraveling from the pins that held it in place. She watches Jacob and Marcel skip to the vending machines, their fingers exploring every possibility even though she has told them already: there is no money for candy, not until they reach the city. She turns to Wilbur, who stands behind her, steady as a signpost.

"You think we're making a mistake?" she asks, voice low enough to avoid the wind.

Wilbur looks at her, then at the bus, then at the horizon. "If it is, it's our mistake to make." He touches her elbow, the gesture so brief it is easy to miss.

She nods, not satisfied but willing to accept the verdict.

Back on the bus, the children's energy has doubled, fueled by the promise of motion and the sudden, dazzling array of sights outside the window: a herd of deer in a ditch, a water tower shaped like a lemon, a man in a suit walking the shoulder of the highway as if he owns it. Each new marvel is announced in a stage whisper, then debated, then added to the running tally of Things We Have Seen.

Mary Lee does not participate, but her eyes flicker each time a new item is named, as if she is building a ledger in her own mind. When Craig reaches over the aisle to point out a cluster of wild turkeys, Mary Lee snaps, "Keep your voice down, you'll wake the whole bus," even though the only people awake are their own.

The hours accrue, sticky and relentless. The air inside the bus is now a solid, oppressive heat, tinged with the sweetness of spilled soda and the underlying note of old sweat. Marcel complains of nausea; Jacob rolls his eyes and calls him a baby, then vomits spectacularly into the paper bag his mother shoves into his lap. The driver does not stop, but Mary Lee marches the boys to the back of the bus, wipes their faces with a cloth she keeps in her purse, and returns them to their seats.

Wilbur continues his silent rituals, marking each passing signpost with a nod. When they cross the border into Oklahoma, he nudges Mary Lee and gestures to the "Welcome" billboard, as if the word alone might be a shield against whatever trouble awaits them.

"They say there's better jobs out here," he offers, not because he believes it, but because it is the necessary thing to say.

Mary Lee does not reply, but she makes a small note in her ledger, the pencil darting over the page like a needle.

At the next stop, a bigger depot with benches and a soda fountain, Craig takes the boys inside for a treat. He hands each a nickel and instructs them to buy whatever they want, so long as it is "not too sticky." He lingers by the magazine rack, pretending to read, but his eyes never leave the entrance. When the boys return—Jacob triumphant with a grape soda, Marcel solemn with a pack of black licorice—Craig lines them up, wipes their mouths, and guides them back to the bus.

Mary Lee, watching from the bench, allows herself a half-smile. She pulls Beth aside and points to a diner across the street, the sign in the window boasting "Best Pie West of the Mississippi."

"You think we have time?" Beth asks, wary.

"We have time if I say we have time," Mary Lee replies. She leads the way, the girls following in her wake.

Inside, the diner is empty except for a tired-looking waitress and a man at the counter who does not look up from his coffee. The girls slide into a booth, and Mary Lee orders three slices of pie —pecan for herself, apple for Beth, and a chocolate cream for sharing.

The pie is mediocre, but it is sweet, and the crust is good. Mary Lee eats hers in small, careful bites, eyes scanning the street outside, checking the bus, the driver, the movement of strangers.

"You think the boys'll be alright?" Beth asks, voice low.

"They're fine. Craig has them."

Afterward, they walk back to the depot, the girls in step, the world outside just beginning to bake in the afternoon sun. When they reboard, the driver eyes them with something like suspicion, but says nothing. The boys are already installed, Jacob reading a comic book, Marcel staring out the window, lost in whatever world he is building for himself.

The road west is a study in exhaustion: miles of flat, then sudden hills, then back to flat again, as if the earth itself cannot make up its mind. The sun slides behind clouds, the light turns blue and metallic, and inside the bus the passengers doze in fits, heads lolling against the glass or each other.

Mary Lee does not sleep. She remains upright, spine unyielding, fingers tracing the seam of her skirt with a rhythm that matches the pulse of the engine.

Wilbur, beside her, finally succumbs to sleep, his head tilting onto his own shoulder, the lines of his face relaxing in the half-light. Mary Lee glances at him, then at the children, then at the world outside. She thinks of the home they have left, of the field and the heat and the brutal familiarity of it all. She thinks of the city waiting for them, of the promise and the peril, the stories she has heard and the ones she cannot yet imagine.

At dusk, the bus pulls into a rest stop outside of Amarillo. The passengers file out, blinking in the harsh light, stretching limbs and blinking eyes. The boys make a beeline for the bathrooms; Beth trails after, moving with a limp she tries to hide. Wilbur stands beside the bus, arms folded, watching the horizon.

Mary Lee joins him, not speaking. They stand together, the wind rifling their clothes, the last rays of sun staining the world a deep, impossible red.

"You think we'll make it?" Wilbur asks.

"We'll make it," Mary Lee says. "We have to."

He nods, accepting the answer.

She looks back at the bus, at the children, at the thin line of highway leading west. She sees in it all the outline of a future—blurred, unsteady, but moving, always moving, toward something else.

When the bus doors open, she gathers her family with a gesture, leads them back inside, and claims their seats. The driver waits until every body is accounted for, then guns the engine, launching them once again into the unknown.

As the night falls, the world outside turns to ink, the only landmarks the periodic flash of headlights, the distant outline of mountains, the faint and holy hum of wheels on pavement. Inside, the children finally sleep, their heads together, the tension of the day melted by fatigue and the promise of arrival.

Mary Lee remains vigilant, her eyes never quite closing, her mind working through the arithmetic of what must come next. She clutches her ledger, the rag, the last tokens of the life left behind. She wills herself not to cry, not to falter.

In the dark, Craig's voice comes from the seat behind: "You rest, Miss Payton. We're almost there."

She does not answer. She simply watches the world unspool beyond the glass, the stars wheeling overhead, the road carrying them forward, forward, into a country she is determined to conquer or die trying.

The bus never really stops, not even when it shudders into a rest area or a roadside diner, not even when it empties its load of souls into the sodium-lit hollows of motels or greasy-spoon restaurants at the margins of towns. The journey is a single, unbroken thread, each mile stitched to the next by the friction of rubber and the machinery of progress. Sleep comes in tatters; meals are measured by the hour, not the appetite. Only the children keep time, marking each stop by the color of the plates and the shape of the coins in their pockets.

The bus pulls over overnight at a roadside lodge, just past Albuquerque; the desert chill seeped into every cinderblock. The room is not just a room, but a kingdom—two beds, a rattling radiator, and a television so ancient it only receives a single channel. Wilbur and Beth claim the first bed, the boys the second, and Mary Lee installs herself in the armchair.

In the morning, the family decamps to the diner across the parking lot, a squat building with a pink neon sign and a jukebox that repeats the same three songs until the cook smacks it with a spatula. The air inside is thick with grease and the low, persistent drone of cross-country truckers. The waitress—White, hair in a helmet of shellac—calls them "hon" without hesitation, takes their order, and brings their food with a smile that lands just short of sincerity.

Jacob and Marcel, seated at the counter between Wilbur and Craig, do not know how to act. They stare at the other customers —a mix of Whites and Mexicans, a Navajo man with a badge on his jacket, two Black boys in matching school uniforms—

waiting for someone to say something, to point out the error in the seating, to send them to the back. No one does. When the food arrives, they eat in silence, the pancakes pale as their palms, the syrup too thin, the butter a cold, hard memory of home.

It is only when Marcel gets up to use the bathroom and comes back wide-eyed that the moment fully lands. "There's no Colored bathroom," he says, his voice trembling with the force of the realization. "We just... go in there?"

Mary Lee answers without looking up from her coffee. "Yup." But her fingers tighten around the mug, knuckles going pale against the ceramic.

Craig watches the boys, his expression shifting between pride and something harder to name—a wariness that never quite leaves his eyes. He tells them to finish quick, then leads them outside, pointing out the mountains in the distance. "Sangre de Cristo," he says, pronouncing the name with a care that borders on reverence, then hesitates. "Means 'blood of Christ.' See how the tops go pink when the sun's low?" The boys squint into the light, and Jacob nods, though his eyes dart back toward the diner door, as if waiting for someone to come out and tell them they've made a terrible mistake.

After some time, the bus pulls into a lunch stop at a highway junction, the only eatery a boxy place run by a couple whose laughter is so loud it drowns out the radio. The tables are mismatched, the menus hand-written, but the food is good— real, generous, heavy. Wilbur orders fried chicken for the table, and when the platter arrives, he waits for everyone to take a piece before serving himself.

The White family at the next table stares for a long minute, then resumes their meal, the children sneaking glances over their mashed potatoes. Mary Lee registers the looks, but does not flinch. She eats with composure, eyes fixed on her plate, every gesture as measured as a prayer.

During the meal, a trucker in a stained jumpsuit comes to their table. He stands over them, uncertain, then clears his throat.

"Excuse me, ma'am," he says to Mary Lee, "but you wouldn't happen to have change for a five?"

She glances at him, then at Wilbur, then at the boys. "We have change," she says. "But you'll have to wait 'til we finish."

The trucker laughs, awkward, and nods. "Sure, sure. Take your time."

He waits at the counter, eyes on the window. When Mary Lee finishes, she counts out five singles, folds them crisp, and hands them over with a look that brooks no nonsense.

"Thank you, ma'am," the man says, voice sheepish.

Mary Lee returns to her seat, and only then does she allow herself the smallest smile.

Craig takes the boys outside, where they throw rocks at the edge of a drainage ditch and marvel at how dry the air is, how dust hangs in the light like something solid. He quizzes them on state capitals, on the names of trees and birds, and though they get most answers wrong, he corrects them with patience.

Wilbur stays inside, paying the check and chatting with the owner, a woman who calls him "sir" and tells him she once had a cousin in Little Rock. When he rejoins the family, he is humming, the sound so low it could be mistaken for the engine of the bus.

Next stop: the Arizona border. The bus breaks down at a tiny station where the only things to look at are cactus and the skeleton of a car that's been left to melt in the sun. The kids fan out, inventing games from trash and gravel. Mary Lee takes the opportunity to re-tape the labels on every box, to triple-check the money hidden in her brassiere, to account for every living soul under her command.

Beth sits on a bench, face hidden in a borrowed magazine, legs crossed at the ankle in a posture of practiced patience. She seems at peace here, in the no-man's-land between states, as if the break in motion is the only rest she will ever know.

Wilbur joins her, takes her hand, and for a long time they sit without words, their silence more intimate than any conversation.

Inside the station, Craig finds a wall map and studies it, tracing the route with his finger, lips moving in silent calculation. When Jacob comes in to fetch him, he puts a hand on the boy's shoulder and says, "We're almost there. Just one more day."

Jacob grins, but there's a question in his eyes.

"What's it like, out there?" he asks.

Craig thinks for a second. "Bigger. Louder. People move fast, but they don't see each other the way they do back home."

Jacob nods, and the two return to the others.

At dusk, the bus is repaired, and the journey resumes. The sun sets with a violence that startles even the most stoic passengers, the sky erupting in color, the landscape rendered in silhouette. The children fall asleep with their heads on each other's shoulders, the adults awake, measuring every bump in the road against the horizon that never seems to draw closer.

Finally there was only one night left on the long road to California. The family is installed in a strip-motel room on the edge of nowhere, the neon sign outside buzzing like an insect, the bedsheets scratchy but clean. The children sleep, sprawled and tangled, dreams written in the slackness of their faces. The adults gather in the glow of a single lamp, voices hushed.

Mary Lee is the first to speak. "They'll have chances we never did," she says, voice clipped but fierce. "No more looking over their shoulders every time they walk down a street. No more waiting for someone to tell them where they can sit."

Craig, slumped in the chair, runs a hand over his chin. "Might be new rules, is all. Different kind of trouble."

Mary Lee's jaw sets. "I'll take different. I'll take anything if it means they live past forty."

Wilbur, seated at the window, looks out at the blackness. He speaks without turning. "We just got to get them there. The rest is up to them."

No one says anything for a time.

Beth, standing by the bathroom door, finally breaks the silence. "I'm scared," she says, voice so thin it barely crosses the room. "I'm scared they'll be the only ones like them, and the city will eat them alive."

Mary Lee's answer is immediate. "We didn't come all this way to hide. We show them how to stand up, how to work, how to make themselves too valuable to lose."

The words hang in the air, heavy as a benediction.

Craig nods, conceding the point.

Wilbur closes the curtain, draws it tight. "We start again tomorrow."

They turn off the light, each adult laying awake a little longer than the next, the night alive with the sound of tires on the highway, the flicker of hope and dread too bright to sleep.

In the morning, they rise, dress, and board the bus for the last time. The mountains are a wall of blue shadow, the sky impossibly clear, the city of San Francisco a rumor on the other side of the range.

They do not look back. They do not need to.

It is nearly noon when the bus chokes its last gasp in the belly of San Francisco, the terminal a cavern of echo and vapor, alive with more people than Mary Lee has ever seen. The family collects itself, the boys pinned to the floor by the press of elbows and knees, Beth clutching Marcel's sleeve as if he might be swept away by the tide of strangers.

The world here is not a world at all, but a storm—voices layered in languages she does not know, the ceaseless whine of engines, the scent of brine and exhaust in equal measure. Jacob tries to name the colors of the city but loses count after twenty, each cab and coat and signboard another violence to his senses.

The Golden Gate Bridge arches in the distance, a punctuation mark on the horizon, and the fog that clings to its spines seems to leak into every corner of the city. Mary Lee watches as the boys orient themselves, first to the terminal, then to the streets outside, their heads on swivels, eyes gone huge and wet with hunger for what is next.

Emeryville is not what she expected. The bus deposits them at a stop between a warehouse and a pawn shop, the sidewalk painted with gum and cigarette butts, the sun obscured by a roof of rolling fog. They stand for a moment, a clutch of birds stunned from the sky, before Craig shoulders the biggest bag and gestures up the hill.

"We're three blocks that way," he says. "Apartment's above the hardware store."

Jacob races ahead, but Mary Lee calls him back, voice taut. "We cross as one. Don't get clever now, boy."

They walk in a wedge, Wilbur flanking the left, Craig on the right, the women and children in the center. Every step feels like a test, the sidewalk shifting under their feet, the unfamiliar faces of passersby ricocheting glances—some curious, some indifferent, a few openly appraising. There are Whites here, but also Black men in union jackets, Chinese women pushing carts, a boy who might be Mexican or Italian laughing with a girl who might be both or neither. No one spits. No one looks away.

The hardware store is a relic, its sign cracked and the bell on the door so loud it startles even the adults. The owner, a man with a voice like boiling water, meets them at the stairs and gestures up. "Third floor, all the way at the back. You got the keys?"

Craig nods, produces them from the pocket of his jacket, and leads the way. The stairs are narrow, the steps uneven; the air inside the building is heavy with sawdust, old paint, and the barely-repressed anxiety of too many lives stacked too close together.

The apartment is smaller than the motel room, a pair of bedrooms split by a sliver of kitchen and a living room whose only furniture is a collapsible table and two chairs. The wallpaper peels in fat strips, and the view from the window is a brick wall and a fire escape. Still, it is theirs.

Mary Lee stands in the center of the apartment, hands on hips, measuring the space with her eyes. She directs the children to the bedroom with the better window, tells Beth to unpack the clothes, and sets Wilbur to assembling the cots Craig has scavenged from the Salvation Army. Within ten minutes, the room is transformed: beds made, food unpacked, order imposed on chaos.

Jacob and Marcel press their faces to the window, pointing at the street below, counting cars and dogs and delivery boys in caps. The city is a live thing, never still, never quiet, and every new sound brings them back to the window, hungry for more.

The adults gather in the kitchen, the narrow table barely accommodating them. Craig unpacks a tin of coffee and sets water to boil on the stove. The burner clicks, then ignites with a whoosh, and for a moment the flame is the only sound.

Beth stands behind Wilbur, arms folded. She does not remove her coat.

Craig pours the coffee and slides a cup to Mary Lee. She nods her thanks, then sips, savoring the heat. The others do the same, and for a moment they are a tableau: four adults, bound by blood and circumstance, holding their breath in the face of the new.

Craig is first to break the silence. "It's not much, but it'll hold us until we find something better."

Mary Lee gives a tight smile. "It's fine. We'll manage."

Wilbur sets his cup down, eyes fixed on the steam rising from it. "You think we'll find work soon?"

Craig shrugs. "Automotive plant is hiring. I'll go down tomorrow, see what's what."

Beth walks to the window and looks out, her posture rigid.

The afternoon wanes, the fog outside thickening into a wet, metallic dusk. The boys beg to explore the building, and Mary Lee sends them with a warning: "Don't go bothering the neighbors. And don't touch nothing you can't spell." They laugh, promise, and disappear into the stairwell.

Left alone, the adults drift to their corners. Craig leans against the counter, head bowed. Wilbur unpacks a Bible from the suitcase and sets it on the windowsill. Beth stands in the doorway to the bedroom, watching the city with the same hollow look she wore on the bus.

Mary Lee, alone in the kitchen, opens her ledger and begins to write. She logs every expense, every meal, every hour, as if the act of recording might keep the chaos from leaking in. Her hands move faster here than they did in Arkansas, the numbers more urgent, more alive.

After a while, Wilbur joins her at the table, his hands folded on the wood. He watches her work, the motion of her pen, the set of her jaw.

"We made it," he says, voice so low she almost misses it.

Mary Lee does not look up. "Yes," she replies. "We did."

She closes the ledger, stacks it with care, and looks out at the city, now aglow with streetlights and the promise of everything unknown.

For the first time, she allows herself to hope that this might be enough.

CHAPTER 6

Wilbur stood beside Craig on the edge of the parking lot, both clutching limp brown-bag lunches and squinting at the vast, boxy bulk of the General Motors factory. The air reeked of hot oil and scorched metal; the unrelenting clang of machinery pulsed in Wilbur's chest like a hammer turning in his ribs. Craig shifted his weight, shoulders tight, jaw clenched. "Never seen so many cars in one place," he muttered, voice so low it might've been a prayer. Awe warred with dread behind his eyes.

Wilbur nodded once, stiffly. "Biggest place I ever worked," he said. "We better hope we fit in."

Inside, the factory world yawned wide and swallowed them. Conveyor belts screeched overhead, sparks spit sickly blue light, and men in grease-spattered coveralls elbowed past without a glance. A foreman in a yellow hardhat barked orders so fast Wilbur barely caught them: Craig was shoved toward engine assembly, and Wilbur was herded onto the assembly line installing transmission housings. They traded a fleeting look —fear and doubt flickering across their faces—then each was carried off by the surge of workers.

On the line, Wilbur's calloused hands trembled around the torque wrench. He struggled to seat each gearbox, his thick fingers slipping on oily flanges. Men with clipped Southern accents hooted from behind smoking pipes, calling him "Hillbilly" as he ratcheted screws that refused to catch. Every stubborn bolt felt like an insult to his pride.

Craig fared no better. He fumbled with engine blocks as if they were live wires, dropping gaskets on the slick floor and earning sharp curses from line supervisors. The city-slick workers whispered rapid slang, their sneers a constant reminder he didn't belong. He swallowed his pride and kept at it, but each tightened bolt felt like a confession of incompetence.

By midday their coveralls clung wet and heavy. They ate lunch on a rickety pallet by a silent alley door, the only sound the hiss of steam vents and Wilbur scraping an apple peel across cracked concrete.

"Think we'll ever get the hang of this?" Craig asked, voice raw.

Wilbur wiped sweat from his brow. "Not sure," he admitted. "But mouths still gotta eat."

They trudged back into the roar, each minute wearing them thinner, every bruise a badge of struggle rather than triumph.

One month later, the factory's chaos had not softened. Wilbur was still "Hillbilly" to most, and every transmission he fitted demanded a second pass. Craig's engine station remained a minefield of snapped bolts and impatient supervisors. Neither had earned respect—no friendly nods, no quick jokes. The blistering heat and endless noise ground them down, and the smell of burning metal clung to their skin like a curse.

At lunch they gathered with other isolated Southerners, swapping fearful glances over stale baloney sandwiches and bitter coffee. The work felt unending, their pay meager, and hope a distant echo drowned by the factory's savage song— metal, sweat, and the relentless rhythm of men forced to endure.

One afternoon, Wilbur trudged up the front walk, his shoulders still streaked with the chalky residue of an all-day inventing spree. A cool breeze from the bay set the cottonwood leaves above him to quivering, their tremors chiming with distant factory whistles and car horns—the neighborhood's collective sigh at shift change. He paused to take in the block's precise geometry: neat squares of grass framed by concrete ribbons, porches standing like weary sentries. In Emeryville's steady, blue-collar rhythm, he found an odd kind of comfort. He missed the boundless sweep of the Arkansas sky, but here California's golden light clung to every surface—windowpanes, mailbox flags, each weathered picket.

On the stoop he noticed a damp patch on his work shirt shaped exactly like a dove. Beth would read it as a sign, so he sheltered it with one hand while the other pressed against the painted door, feeling the wood flex. Then he stepped into the half-dark.

Inside, the house was alive with motion. The living-room clock ticked steadily. From the kitchen came the rhythmic chop-chop of Beth's knife working through a pile of collard greens beside a steaming cast-iron skillet. Leaning in the doorway, Wilbur watched her—heels together, hips dipping with each slice. She didn't turn, but when the blade paused for a fraction of a second, he knew she'd heard him.

"Long day?" she asked without facing him.

He tugged at his collar. "Not as long as yours, I'll bet."

Beth snorted. "At least mine comes with flavor." She set the knife down so gently the cutting board barely trembled, wiped her hands on her apron, then turned. Lamplight caught the tired rings beneath her eyes, though the skin around them lay surprisingly smooth—no new scrapes today.

"Craig's coming by after supper," she added, folding her arms. "Says he's got big news."

Wilbur grunted. "I hope it comes with a bigger check, or I don't want to hear it."

Beth's lips curved in a half-smile. "You're not as hard to please as you think." She reached up and smoothed the collar away from his neck; her fingers were cool. He bent close, breathing in the sharp tang of vinegar and iron in her hair, then wrapped his arms around her waist. She bobbed beneath him like a fragile bloom.

After a moment, he murmured against her ear, "You hear from your mother?"

"She called," Beth said quietly. "Wants us to visit her church on Sunday. Said our apartment's too small for hosting, but she'll bring a sheet cake."

Wilbur exhaled and let the hush settle around them—no mention of Sunday suits, hymnal-folding hands, or pews filled with strangers who'd never known callouses. He savored the soft half-light and the quiet anchor of her body in his arms.

Wilbur sighed. "Alright, but just this once."

Behind them, Jacob let out a shrill shriek, then laughter. "Jacob!" Beth called, not loosening her embrace. "Stop hitting your brother. I won't have that in my house."

A pause, then a muffled reply: "He started it."

The days at General Motors settled into routine, the clang of metal and hiss of steam becoming the rhythm of Wilbur's new life. Each paycheck, Wilbur tucked a few dollars deep into a coffee can hidden at the back of the cupboard—rent paid first, groceries second, whatever was left set aside for something more. He counted every nickel, every bruised bill, letting hope grow alongside the secret stash.

By spring, the can was heavy. Wilbur walked the grid of quiet streets after his shift, scanning empty lots until he found one —a patch of rough grass and broken concrete at the edge of

Emeryville, just wide enough for a modest house and a garden. He met the owner, signed the deed with hands still marked by mortar and grease, and paid in careful bills.

That Sunday, he brought Beth and the children to see the lot. The kids ran wild through the weeds, Beth's face caught between disbelief and pride. Wilbur knelt in the dirt, pressed his palm flat to the earth, and promised, "Every brick, every board—gonna lay it myself. This'll be ours."

Beth's fingers dug into the muscle of his shoulder, five points of pressure that said more than words. Her eyes, wet at the corners, moved from the weedy lot to his face, then back again. The corner of her mouth twitched upward, just barely, as she exhaled a breath she might have been holding since Arkansas.

Wilbur nodded, already imagining the straight lines and solid walls—the sturdy, beautiful house that would finally belong to them, built with his own two hands.

Dawn in Emeryville arrives not as a revelation, but as a gradual unbuckling. The night, stitched together by the wheeze of barges and the yowl of feral cats, falls open seam by seam until the bare threads of morning light snag on the broken glass and rebar of the vacant lot. Wilbur is first to claim the day, standing at the perimeter where city sidewalk surrenders to cracked dirt, the ground stitched with the memory of wild mustard and old industrial poison. He breathes in the air, heavy with salt and the undertow of spent gasoline, and feels the prickle of moisture through his shirt—fog, cold and living, anointed by the Pacific.

To the north, the General Motors factory is already awake, its metallic drone braiding with the calls of blackbirds nested in the wires overhead.

He carries his lunch and his tools in separate sacks. Lunch—a baloney sandwich, two apples, thermos of tap water—rides at his side like a necessary vice. Tools go first; he sets them out on a plank of wet plywood, arranges them with the precision of a man laying offerings at an altar. Wilbur runs a fingertip over the row, a silent inspection, then nods once and stands back.

"Showtime," he mutters, not for the tools, not for the factory or the birds, but for the empty grid of stakes and string that waits like a promise. The future home.

He turns, scanning the lot, expecting to see the others—but for ten full minutes, he is alone with the sunrise and the far-off laughter of gulls. Wilbur is grateful for this; alone, he can rehearse his first impression. He squares his cap, brushes the dust from his knees, flexes his fingers until they pop in sequence.

Then the foreman arrives: a tall, pale man with the permanent squint of one who has spent his life fighting the sun. He wears a hardhat like a crown and a windbreaker the color of funeral lilies. He approaches with the shuffle of a man whose back was broken once and never properly fixed. Wilbur notes the limp, the way the man favors his right knee.

"King, right?" the foreman says, skidding a boot in the mud.

Wilbur extends a hand, thumb up, the proper way. "That's me."

"Walt," the man replies, his grip quick and dry, a spark of recognition passing between their palms. "You ever build up from scratch?"

"Yes, sir. Churches. Warehouses. Pig pens."

Walt grins, teeth tobacco-stained but intact. "Heard you got a way with lines."

Wilbur shrugs, but pride floats up in his throat, a bubble he must swallow twice before it goes down. "I do straight, mostly."

"Good. We need straight." Walt gestures to the lot. "You know the plan?"

Wilbur's reply is a short nod, but in his mind he is already rehearsing the blueprint: foundation, slab, cinder block, joist. He spent the night before memorizing the scale, tracing the ghost lines of the architect's drawing onto the ceiling of the apartment, redrafting the measurements in his sleep.

"Set up here," Walt says, kicking a chunk of concrete. "I want the first trench squared by lunch. We're on a fast schedule." He unfurls a sheaf of blueprints across a makeshift table—two sawhorses and a door salvaged from a demolition. The paper flaps in the wind, and Walt anchors it with a coffee can half-filled with nails.

Wilbur leans in, reading the lines not as abstractions but as a set of prayers. "You want the rebar double-lapped at the corners?"

"Absolutely," Walt says, and Wilbur nods again.

The conversation is over; the work begins.

The day unfolds in increments of labor. Wilbur sets the lines first, taut and humming, marking out the rectangle with a patience that would shame a surveyor. Each stake is driven with exactly three swings, no more, no less.

By seven, a second crew arrives—two Chicano men and a kid who cannot be older than fifteen but moves dirt with the desperation of a drowning man. Wilbur clocks their arrival, lifts his chin in greeting, but does not bother with names yet. That will come, or not, according to the laws of proximity and shared suffering.

He spends the morning on his knees, scraping the first trench, smoothing the sides with the edge of his trowel until the dirt is a fine, even plane. His hands know the rhythm; he lets them take over, mind wandering to the memory of other foundations. Texarkana. Little Rock. Even as a boy, building pig sties with his grandfather, learning the gospel of the plumb line and the spirit level.

The air warms, thickens, loses its edge. By noon, Wilbur's shirt is slick at the collar, the sleeves stiff with dry sweat. He eats his sandwich perched on a stack of block, staring out at the haze that blankets the Bay, the cranes and smokestacks in the distance rendered spectral by the rising heat.

Walt checks in at intervals, each time with the same question, "How we looking?" and each time Wilbur answers with a precise number: feet, inches, volume of spoil. After the second check, Walt stops measuring and starts trusting.

"You ever think about being a lead?" Walt asks, eyeing the depth of the trench.

Wilbur shakes his head. "I like the work too much."

Walt nods, as if this is an answer he understands. "Most men want to get off their knees as soon as they can."

Wilbur, brushing his palms clean, says, "I never minded kneeling. It's what you do after that matters."

The foreman laughs, a short cough of sound. "Hell, maybe you should be a preacher."

Wilbur grins, only briefly. "Tried that once. Didn't take."

The rest of the day passes in a kind of fugue—earth, chalk, steel. The forms go up, the rebar is wired and lashed, and by three in the afternoon, the first wheelbarrow of concrete is ready to be poured. Wilbur guides the flow with his trowel, coaxing the mud into corners, feathering it along the edge so it will set with no voids or air pockets. The sun creeps lower, tinting the lot in gold and pink, the city's noise growing louder but further away.

When the first course of block is laid, Walt comes over, crouches at eye level, and runs a finger along the joint.

"Damn," he says. "That's a pretty seam."

Wilbur shrugs, but again, the pride is impossible to deny. He wants to say: I am building something that will outlast my bones. Instead, he dips his brush in the water pail and wipes the line clean, careful to leave no mess for the next day.

By sunset, the foundation is visible—a low, precise skeleton rising from the earth, the outlines of rooms and doorways already clear to anyone who knows how to look. Wilbur stands back, shoulders caked with dust, the ache in his back an old, reliable friend. The kid from the morning crew has vanished, but the two older men linger, sharing a can of warm beer on the tailgate of a truck. They have at him to join. Wilbur ignores the invitation; his reward is the silence and the shadow of what's to come.

He washes at the communal spigot, the water frigid, stinging the cuts and cracks in his skin. He scrubs the mortar from his wrists, the chalk from his knuckles, and watches the slurry spiral down the gutter to the storm drain. When he is clean, he dries his hands on the thighs of his jeans, takes a last long look at the day's work, and lets out a breath he did not know he was holding.

The street is empty now, the city settling into its evening. Wilbur shoulders his sack of tools, feeling their weight with a satisfaction almost religious, and heads homeward, following the sidewalk past the chain link fence, past the whistle of the factory and the echo of his own footfalls.

He thinks of the rooms that will rise on this lot: bedrooms, kitchen, maybe even a parlor with a view of the lake, if the money holds out. He thinks of Beth and the boys, of the promise he made to bring them to a place where every nail is driven straight and every wall stands true.

He walks slow, savoring the fatigue. It is the good kind, earned and honest, the kind that lingers like a blessing.

When he reaches the apartment, Beth is there in the window, framed by the glow of a single lamp. She watches him approach, her silhouette unbroken. Wilbur lifts a hand in greeting, and she lifts hers in return.

In the last light, the world seems briefly held together by the thin line of his arm, the faint gleam of wet brick, the knowledge that—if only for a day—the line held straight, the corner did not give, and the walls stood firm against the dark.

Beth sits at the rickety table by the window of the apartment, spine pinched by the back of a borrowed chair, and types with determination. The keys on the old Smith-Corona require more force than expected, each strike a minor violence, and the ribbon —rescued from the trash behind the post office—fades after half a page, so that she must go back, fill in the ghosts with a pen. It is tedious, but not as tedious as the silence that threatens when she stops.

The letter is a petition, a choreography of need and assertion, the kind that must sound urgent but not desperate. She is writing to the matron of the orphanage in Texarkana to assure them that Angelique, Isaiah and Alphonse will be met at the station, that there is a home and work and school waiting, that their kin are not rootless or shiftless or liable to be a burden. She practices the sentences aloud before she types them, paring away every "um" and "well" and "just," so that what is left is a clean, sharp plea.

She pauses to read back:

"Dear Mrs. Everett: This is to confirm that my husband Wilbur King and I, formerly of Miller County, will be in receipt of our children Angelique, Isaiah and Alphonse by June 14th, 1968. We have stable residence and employment, and the children's transition will not present any hardship to your institution. Please advise if there are additional forms to complete, or if you require a notary for the custody transfer. Sincerely, Beth King (née Payton)."

She blots the signature, refolds the letter, and slides it into an envelope already addressed, her handwriting upright and defiant. She licks the flap, presses it closed, and sets it at the edge of the table.

The table itself is scarred with the history of other tenants: burns, knife marks, the trace of someone's initials gouged so deep the wood splinters. Beth covers it with a dish towel before every meal, but in the evenings she leaves it bare, as if to remind herself that nothing here is permanent. Every time she leans forward, she can feel the old wounds digging into her forearms, a geography of sorrow that cannot be sanded away.

She listens: upstairs, a man plays the trumpet, badly. Next door, a baby wails, and the mother's voice rises over it, a string of words in Spanish that are alternately sweet and blistering. Below, someone bangs a pipe in what must be a coded signal for the landlord, but the landlord is never around at this hour. The walls are thin as paper; Beth can hear the neighbors' grief and pleasure as clearly as her own thoughts. Sometimes she cannot tell which is which.

At the other end of the apartment, Marcel and Jacob sit on the pull-out sofa, their knees pressed together, hunched over a game of dominoes. Marcel is losing badly, but he refuses to admit it; Jacob, sensing his brother's pride, lets him win a round now and then, stacking the dominoes with deliberate care so that they topple in a line. When the last tile falls, they both sigh, a brief truce in their campaign of one-upmanship.

Beth watches them without appearing to do so, her eyes

flickering from the letter to the boys to the clock, measuring every second. Wilbur will be late tonight; the first day of a new site always runs long, especially if the foreman is the kind to double-check every measurement. She has told herself not to worry, but the habit is older than her marriage. She worries anyway.

With the letter finished, she opens the coffee tin, counts out the quarters, dimes, and nickels—separated by denomination and rolled tight in bank sleeves. She keeps a ledger, just like her mother, each transaction recorded in minuscule script: groceries, rent, postage, school fees, the cost of the pay phone, the cost of the streetcar, the cost of the new shoes Jacob will need by fall. She totals the balance twice, then a third time for luck.

Four dollars and seventy-three cents will not buy much, but it will cover the tickets to San Francisco, and perhaps leave enough for a sweet at the station when the children arrive. Beth makes a note in the margin—"Angelique, lemon drops; Alphonse, peppermint stick"—then closes the ledger with a click.

She is ready. She has always been ready, even when she was not.

The hardest part is the phone call. Beth hates the phone—its imprecision, its demand for quick answers, its trick of making her voice sound small and scratchy. She prefers letters: letters can be rewritten, letters can be controlled. But there is no avoiding the call. Mrs. Everett expects it, and the ticket agent at the station will not reserve the children's seats unless a real voice confirms the arrangement.

She bundles her coat, tucks the envelope and ledger under her arm, and tells the boys to stay put until Wilbur gets home. She leaves the apartment, locking it twice, and walks the three blocks to the corner store, where a pay phone hangs between two pinball machines. She buys a pack of gum from the cashier, to make the visit legitimate, then waits for the man ahead of her to finish. He talks so loud Beth can hear every word: a fight with his girlfriend, a question about payday, a string of laughter that rattles the handset. When he leaves, he does not meet her eyes, but she can smell his cologne, cheap and electric, trailing behind him like a warning.

Beth dials the number from the letter. Her fingers are numb at first, but the muscle memory takes over. She listens to the ring, then the click as Mrs. Everett answers, her voice crisp and businesslike.

"Good afternoon, Texarkana Children's Home."

"Hello, this is Beth King. I'm calling about the travel arrangements for my children, Angelique, Isaiah and Alphonse. We received the itinerary, and I wanted to confirm the pickup at the Little Rock station."

There is a pause, the faint scratch of pen on paper. "Yes, Mrs. King, we have you down for the fifteenth of June. Are you still at the same address?"

"Yes, ma'am. The boys and I are in San Francisco now—Emeryville, specifically. We'll be meeting them at the depot in Oakland."

"Fine, fine. And the tickets? Will you be purchasing them in advance, or should we handle the fare on our end and be reimbursed?"

Beth's voice is steady, but her knuckles whiten on the receiver. "I have the funds. I'll send the check tomorrow."

"Very good. The children are in good health, no behavioral issues to report. Angelique helps with the younger ones, and Alphonse keeps to himself, but no trouble. You should be proud."

Beth closes her eyes, lets the words fill her up. "Thank you, ma'am. I appreciate your care."

After the call, she stands in the vestibule for a long moment, breathing in the scent of bubble gum and ammonia, her head pressed against the cool glass. She is relieved, and yet something in her chest feels unmoored, as if the certainty of the arrangement has made the whole world less stable.

She walks home with her chin tucked into her coat, thinking about how she will tell Wilbur the news.

That night, after dinner—canned soup and toast, with a treat of tinned peaches for dessert—Beth sits at the table and writes a second letter, this one to Angelique and Alphonse. She chooses her words with care, conscious of the smallness of the space and the largeness of what must be said:

"Dearest children,

Your father and I are counting the days until you arrive. We have a room ready, and the school here is very fine. Jacob and Marcel are eager to show you the city, and I cannot wait to braid Angelique's hair myself, no more tangles, no more fuss. Your daddy is working hard to build us a home of our own. We love you, and we will be waiting at the station, rain or shine.

All my love,

Mama."

She folds the letter, tucks in a snapshot of the boys—Jacob grinning, Marcel scowling, both in their best shirts—and seals the envelope.

She lingers over the return address, printing each letter in capital block, so that the postman cannot mistake it. She wants the letter to arrive. She needs it to.

Wilbur comes home late, face smudged with concrete dust, eyes rimmed in red. He looks at the boys first, then at Beth, and sits across from her with a heaviness that sags the table.

She tells him the news: the tickets, the confirmation, the date and time. Wilbur nods, silent, then rubs his hand over his scalp, as if to make sure it is still attached.

He says, "You did good," and Beth feels the warmth of it, even if he cannot say more.

They sit together as the city quiets around them, the trumpeter upstairs finally yielding to sleep, the baby next door pacified, the pipe-banging man giving up for the night. The silence is a different kind now—less hostile, more a space in which to gather themselves.

Beth counts the letters one last time, stacks them in order, and places the tickets inside the envelope. She smooths the flap, runs her palm over the paper, and holds it up to the last light coming through the window.

Her shadow stretches long across the floor, angular and unbending. She lets it stay there, a silhouette of all she has left behind and all she is determined to claim.

In the morning, she will take the letters to the post office herself. She will buy a lemon drop for Angelique, a peppermint stick for Alphonse, and maybe—if the world is kind—a licorice twist for herself.

But for now, there is this: the knowledge that her children are coming home, that she has made a way for them, that nothing in this new city is permanent but the love she has fought to preserve.

She sits at the table, ledger open, tickets safe, and lets the future find her.

The train has barely stopped shuddering when Angelique opens the door and steps out, suitcase already dangling from her wrist, the other hand snagging Isaiah and Alphonse's sleeves so they do not wander, not yet. The air on the platform is alive—alive in a way she's never felt, not in Arkansas, not in any of the places the train passed. It is cold, first of all, but a bright cold, the kind that pulls your breath in and wrings it out, so every word you say floats in the air for a second before it vanishes. Angelique takes a test inhale, then another, and her whole head floods with the scent of salt, steel, and the odd, sharp edge of something burning in the distance—maybe tar, maybe food.

Alphonse stands beside her, the cardboard suitcase pressed to his belly, eyes narrowed at the mess of people unloading from other cars. He says nothing, but she can tell he's counting, cataloging, marking which ones are White, which are Black, which are nothing he can name.

The platform is a circus: women in hats and gloves, men with cigars clamped in their teeth, a boy with hair so white it looks powdered. There are more Black folks here than Angelique expected, but none of them sound right when they talk—some speak Spanish, some another language she can't place, some just fast, like every word is a dare.

She tries to stand tall, tries to look like she's been here before, but her knees are loose.

Beth is easy to spot, even in the crowd. She stands near the baggage window, hands on hips, scarf tied just so. Her face is thinner, the shadows under her eyes deeper, but she is here, and that is all that matters.

Angelique does not run to her. Instead, she marches across the platform, Alphonse trailing like a tugboat, and stops one step shy of contact.

"Hi, Mama," she says, and hears her own voice thin and sharp in the cold.

Beth's hug is quick, hard, all bone and no cushion, but it is real.

She does not cry, does not even blink; she just says, "You made good time," and takes both suitcases with one hand, the other gathering Alphonse in and steering him toward the exit.

They walk fast, Mama setting the pace, through the terminal where every step echoes. The station here is bigger than anything back home, and Angelique stares at the chandeliers, the painted ceiling, the crowds that part and close like the Red Sea. She wants to look everywhere at once, but Mama keeps a grip on her shoulder.

Alphonse says nothing. Angelique glances at him—his face has that look he gets when he's about to be sick, a gray cast that makes him look like he belongs to a different family.

"You okay?" she whispers.

He nods, then shakes his head. "It's loud," he says.

She squeezes his fingers. "We just got to get outside. It'll be better."

Outside is no better, but it is at least different. The fog is thick enough to catch in her eyelashes, and the air feels like it's made of silk and ice at the same time. The city is loud, yes, but it's not the honking and shouting of home. It's a hum, a buzz, a constant, relentless shifting that she thinks must go all the way down to the bones of the ground.

They reach the curb, and Mama stops, scanning the row of cars and trucks until she spots an old Ford pickup idling by the corner. She marches over, knocks on the glass, and the driver— a Black man, hair close-cropped, smile quick—leans across and pops the door.

"Mr. Fred," she says, and he tips his hat.

"In you go, Miss Beth. I see you found your ducklings."

The three of them pile in, Angelique pressed against the window,

Alphonse in the middle. The truck smells like old tobacco and lemon oil, but it is warm, and the seat is soft after so many hours on the train.

"First time in California?" Fred asks, pulling away from the curb.

"Yes, sir," Angelique says. She is determined to answer for both of them.

"You're gonna like it," he says. "No snow, no chiggers, and you can buy oranges by the sack."

Alphonse perks up at that, but Mama shoots Fred a look, and he quiets. Angelique knows Mama doesn't like the kids thinking things will be easy, but she doesn't care—she wants the oranges, wants the sky and the water and everything this city promises.

They drive, the truck rattling over every seam in the street. The world outside is a blur: factories, stores, whole neighborhoods stacked on hills like steps to heaven. She sees a school, a playground with children running, a man selling newspapers at a stand that looks like it will fall over in the wind.

She glances at Mama, waiting for her to say something, but her face is closed, set in a way Angelique knows not to challenge.

It takes twenty minutes to reach the edge of Emeryville, and another ten to find the lot. Mr. Fred parks on a patch of gravel across from a long fence, the kind made of chain link and crowned with barbed wire. There is nothing pretty about the place, but the air is cleaner here, and the sound of the city is muffled by the distance.

Angelique sees Wilbur before anyone else does. He stands in the shadow of the half-built house, hands on his hips, eyes narrowed against the sun. His shirt is off, the white of his undershirt glowing in the twilight, and his skin glistens with sweat and cement dust. He is taller than she remembers, but more stooped, like the work is pulling him downward, pressing him into the ground he is trying to build on.

When he spots them, his face splits in a grin—not wide, not showy, but real. He wipes his hands on his pants, then strides over, arms open. Angelique steps into the hug, burying her nose in the crease of his shoulder. He smells like salt and old leather, the same as always.

"You did good," he whispers, squeezing her so hard she can barely breathe.

He turns to Alphonse, ruffles his hair.

Alphonse nods, shy at first, but when Wilbur leads them across the lot, he follows without looking back.

The house is nothing yet: three walls, a partial roof, the floor just a scatter of plywood and nails. But Angelique can see it, can see the lines of the rooms, the bones of the place that will be theirs. Wilbur explains each part as they walk, tapping the studs and beams, showing where the kitchen will go, where the bedrooms will be.

"This here," he says, pointing to a gap in the floor, "is where the fireplace will be. We'll build it strong, so the whole place stays warm all winter."

Angelique touches the wood, the splinters rough under her palm. She tries to imagine the walls painted, the windows hung with curtains, the table set for supper. It is hard, but she tries.

Wilbur leads them outside, to where the first course of bricks is already set. The mortar is still damp, the bricks red and perfect. He kneels, pats the spot beside him, and waits until Angelique and Alphonse crouch down too.

"See this line?" he says, running a finger over the seam between two bricks. "That's what you look at when you're laying the next row. If it's straight, the whole wall will be straight. If it's crooked, the whole house goes funny."

He takes Angelique's hand, sets it on the brick, then does the same for Alphonse. Their hands are smaller than his, but strong.

"You do it," he says. "Run your finger across."

They do. Angelique feels the grit of the mortar, the coolness of the brick, the slight give where the line isn't perfect.

"Why's it matter?" Alphonse asks.

Wilbur thinks about this for a moment. "If you get the first part right, you can fix anything that comes after. If you don't, you spend the rest of your life trying to make up for it."

Angelique nods, understanding more than she can say.

They eat supper on the tailgate of the truck—beans from a can, white bread, and a pint of buttermilk to split. Mama sits beside them, legs crossed at the ankle, eyes on the house. Wilbur brings over a tin cup of water, sets it next to Angelique, and nods his thanks to Fred, who lights a cigarette and leans against the fender, content to watch.

The food is gone too fast, but the company lasts. The sun sets slow over the city, painting the half-built house in gold. Angelique listens as Wilbur tells stories about the jobs he's had— the time a wall fell down and nearly took him with it, the time he built a church so solid even the preacher couldn't complain. She can tell he is proud, even if he never says so.

Alphonse wanders away, circling the lot. He comes back with a rock shaped like an arrowhead, which he shows to Wilbur with a shy grin.

"You got an eye," Wilbur says.

Alphonse grins wider, then tucks the rock in his pocket.

When it's time to go, Mama stands and brushes the crumbs from her skirt. She gathers the suitcases, then takes Angelique's hand.

"Say goodbye to your daddy," she says.

Angelique does, but not for long. She knows they will see him tomorrow, and the day after, and every day until the house is done.

In the truck, on the way to the house, Angelique leans against the window, watching the lights flicker past. She is tired, but more than that, she is hungry—for the oranges, for the house, for the day when she will not have to start over again.

Beside her, Alphonse is already asleep, the rock in his fist.

Angelique lets her eyes close, but not all the way. She wants to remember every part of this day, even the hard bits.

Back at the house, Mama tucks them into the fold-out bed. The springs squeak, but the blanket is warm, and the room smells like soap and cinnamon. Mama kisses their foreheads, then turns out the light.

In the dark, Angelique whispers, "Did you like it? The house?"

Alphonse is quiet for a long time. Then he says, "It's not done yet."

Angelique smiles. "Neither are we."

The house, the city, the whole world—none of it finished, all of it waiting.

She closes her eyes, and dreams of brick, of straight lines, of walls that never fall down.

CHAPTER 7

With the family reunited, the Kings never had quite enough, not with what Wilbur brought home. Rent ate most of it, groceries the rest, leaving nothing for extras—certainly not the fresh fruit that gleamed in market stalls, just out of reach. Jacob's stomach twisted as he followed his siblings toward Mrs. Gutierrez's yard. "We shouldn't," he whispered, even as his mouth watered at the thought of plums. Marcel shot him a look that silenced further protest.

The alley lay in half-shadow as four silhouettes approached the fence. Marcel's arms strained as he boosted Alphonse up, fingers digging into the younger boy's ankles. At the top, Alphonse froze, eyes darting between the laden branches and the ground below. "What if she calls the police?" he hissed. "What if Mama finds out?" But hunger won, and he disappeared over. On lookout, Angelique's fingers trembled against Jacob's sleeve. A breeze rustled through the plum trees and Jacob startled, his mother's voice suddenly in his head: "I raised you better." Yet when Angelique's apron returned sagging with purple bounty, he was the first to reach for a fruit, the sweetness on his tongue both heaven and accusation.

The back door slammed. A shrill cry tore through the alley—Mrs. Gutierrez, broom in hand, fury in her voice. "¡Ladrones! I know your mamá!" The world tilted as the children dropped plums in their scramble over the fence, juice smearing their wild escape. Jacob's chest pounded with the sudden weight of fear and remorse.

They hadn't gone far when word raced ahead of them. At home, Beth stood waiting, face drawn tight as wire. No soft words, no questions—just an arm yanked forward. The first crack of her belt made Jacob's stomach lurch. Each strike rang through the hallway like judgment. Angelique threw herself over Alphonse, but Beth's fury cared nothing for mercy. The strap landed on Angelique's forearm, and her gasp sounded like a challenge. "I will not have thieves in my house—do you hear me?" she hissed. Shame burned hotter than the belt's sting; tears mingled with the sticky residue still clinging to their skin.

Beth marched them back to Mrs. Gutierrez's porch in a grim procession, shoulders hunched against humiliation. Words of apology trembled on their lips while they returned the few salvaged plums. Beth stood over them, muttering about shame, about hunger, about a world that punished thievery without pity. Only when the last apology was uttered did she let them retreat, leaving each child to haul their wounded pride homeward.

On the walk to the lake, the ache of Beth's blows trailed them —heavy as guilt, sharper than that plum's sweetness. Jacob's ears buzzed with shame; each rattling leaf seemed to whisper reminders of their theft. Angelique limped forward, rubbing the welt on her arm, grinning as if pain were another prize to win. Alphonse lagged, diving curious fingers into bulging dungarees to trace the bruise on his thigh, as though studying a mystery. Marcel strode ahead, sleeves rolled up to show off his biceps, pushing back the guilt with swagger Jacob knew was purely for show.

From the water's edge, Emeryville felt alien. The warehouses loomed half-swallowed by fog, as if the city itself was trying to hide its scars. Wild fennel crowded against the grass, brittle stalks scratching at ankles. The lake was polluted with trash and rusted carts below the surface. Jacob shivered, wondering if guilt weighed as heavily down there.

Under the scant shade of a stunted willow, they assembled their makeshift gear. Rods of salvaged fencing wire cut and bound with blue electrical tape, bottle-cork floats bobbing on twine. Angelique cranked her old reel the wrong way twice before it grudgingly spun. Marcel hacked roofing nails into hooks, each clang making Jacob's nerves twinge. When Marcel plucked a raisin from his pocket, halved it, and skewered the pulp, Jacob thought he saw doubt cross his brother's face—just for a second.

"Gonna catch something bigger than you," Marcel boasted, flicking his line out with practiced ease. Yet Jacob held his breath, torn between hoping for a fish and fearing it might be the one thing he didn't deserve.

Angelique grunted. "Just don't lose the string again."

While the others bickered over bait and casting, Jacob cupped his palms into the cold drift of water at his feet, watching the ripples shiver away. The memory of Mrs. Gutierrez's yell echoed in his chest—your mama!—as if the whole city was appointed to keep them in line. He tried to remember the last time Beth had looked at him with anything less than tiredness. He couldn't.

Jacob tested the depth of the water with a stick, poking at dark shapes just below the surface. "The catfish sleep in the shade. We have to wait until they come out."

"Who says we're catching catfish?" Marcel said, peeling a strip of plum skin from his palm.

A car honked above on the overpass—three sharp notes, then a curse word trailing in its wake. Jacob looked up and caught the flash of chrome, the movement of someone peering over the railing. For a second, he thought it was Beth, come to check on them, but the figure was gone before he could be sure.

Angelique's cork bobbed once, violently, then vanished. She jerked the line hard, wrenching a fat bluegill from the lake. The fish thrashed against the mud, scales iridescent in the sun.

"Jesus, it's huge," Marcel said, voice suddenly high.

Angelique beamed, holding the line up for all to see. "Big enough to eat," she announced.

Alphonse looked at the fish, then at Jacob, then down again. "Ain't hungry," he said. But Jacob knew he was.

The sun slid behind the warehouses, stretching their shadows across the lake. Jacob's line went slack for the fifth time.

"Nothing's biting," Marcel muttered, yanking his empty hook from the water.

Angelique shook her empty tin. "We're out."

They fanned out along the water's edge, fingers probing the soft earth. Marcel unearthed a pink, writhing tangle. Alphonse pocketed something white and curved—last summer's bird, picked clean. The cattails swayed, their brown heads nodding in the breeze that rippled the water's surface.

Jacob stopped at a patch of dark soil. "Here," he said, jamming his rod into the silt. The others gathered without being told, a formation practiced over countless afternoons.

"Watch it," Angelique said, pointing to where mud bubbled at the shore's edge. She pinched her skirt between two fingers, lifting the hem an inch above the muck. "Remember last month, Marcel? When you—"

"Shut up," Marcel flashed a crooked grin.

"Daddy said one more pair of shoes and you're barefoot till Christmas." Angelique knelt on higher ground, sweeping aside dead leaves with the edge of her hand, each movement precise as stitches.

Alphonse dug his screwdriver into the clay, twisting it with both hands, his tongue caught between his teeth.

Jacob produced a rusted tin from inside his jacket. "Worms," he said, rattling it. "Who's digging?"

"Not me," said Angelique, but her eyes flicked to Marcel, who was already on his knees, mud squishing between his fingers.

Jacob pressed the can into Marcel's palm, then bent close to his ear. "Go deep," he whispered. "Fat ones hide at the bottom." His eyes darted to the trees, scanning for shadows that didn't belong.

Marcel stabbed at the ground, then paused to measure with his thumb. "Should've brought the trowel."

"Real men use their hands," Jacob said. Marcel looked down at his dirt-streaked palms, then back at Jacob's face, his jaw tightening.

Angelique wandered ten paces away, studying the shoreline. "Over there," she called, pointing to a slick of obsidian-colored mud. "See how wet it is? That's where they'll be."

Jacob's nostrils flared, but he said nothing, just jerked his chin toward the spot. He'd seen the glint in her eye that meant she was right.

Alphonse edges closer to the spot, watching the others from beneath his brow. "I found a clam shell," he announces, holding up the cracked white fragment. "Big one."

"Don't eat it," Angelique says. "You'll die."

Alphonse grins. "Maybe I want to."

Jacob snorts. "You're so weird."

"I'm just saying, if you're gonna die, do it fast. Not like that dog at the dump."

The memory hangs for a moment—the way the world

sometimes refuses to be kind, even to the least of its inhabitants.

Marcel breaks the tension, shoving a fistful of worms into the can. "Enough yet?"

"Not even close," says Jacob. "It's four rods, four times the bait. Angelique, help him."

She hesitates, then kneels beside Marcel, careful to keep her fingers clean as she sifts through the clumps he loosens.

They work in silence, the only sound the plop of mud and the far-off caw of a crow. For a moment, they are four bodies bent to a single purpose, the world shrunk to the stubborn yield of earth.

When the can is half full, Jacob claims it and sets about baiting the lines. His hands are quick, decisive, the movements practiced from years of small-town boredom and the need to produce. He loops the worms just so, never too tight, never so loose they'll slip off with the first tug. He shows the knot to Angelique, who nods, then to Marcel, who pretends not to care.

Alphonse watches the whole process, eyes following Jacob's hands as if memorizing each step for later theft.

Jacob plants the first rod, then the next, spacing them for maximum coverage. "You can't crowd them," he explains, "or they just scare each other off."

Angelique raises an eyebrow. "Who told you that?"

"It's true. Ask anyone who's fished here."

"I bet you just want all the good spots for yourself." But there's no bite in her voice.

Marcel sets his rod, then sits on the bank, hands muddy and drying in the sun. "I heard this lake has a bottomless part," he says. "You fall in, you don't come out."

"That's a lie," says Angelique. "It's not even five feet deep."

"Some parts are. The rest is deep as hell." Marcel makes a dramatic gesture with his arms. "There's cars down there. Even a dead guy."

Jacob grins. "If you go in, I'll pull you out by your feet. Then we can check if your head's full of water."

Marcel flips him off, casual and almost affectionate.

Alphonse moves closer to the water, peering in. "There's something shiny down there," he says, voice low. "Look."

Angelique approaches, her reflection sharp on the surface. "Where?"

"Right there," says Alphonse, pointing. "Something metal. Maybe a coin."

Jacob shoves past the others, squinting. "It's probably just trash."

But he leans in, and for a moment, all four are huddled at the edge, eyes straining to see what the lake is willing to reveal.

An hour passes. They catch nothing, but the rods twitch now and then, a false hope that keeps them anchored to the mud. Jacob checks each line, adjusts the weights, makes small corrections with the confidence of an oldest child.

Marcel grows bored, starts digging with a stick, carving his name in the clay. Angelique braids a length of grass, then unbraids it, fingers restless.

Alphonse stares at the water, still fixated on the flash of metal beneath the surface.

"I bet it's a ring," he says. "Like from a dead gangster."

Angelique rolls her eyes. "What would a gangster be doing out here?"

"Burying a body," says Marcel. "Duh."

"Shut up, you're scaring Alphonse."

Alphonse grins. "I'm not scared. Maybe I'll dig it up."

Jacob, overhearing, tosses a pebble at Alphonse's back. "Stay away from the edge, stupid. You'll fall in."

Alphonse ignores him, but the warning is understood.

A breeze kicks up, ruffling the surface of the lake. The sun slides lower, turning the water to a sheet of molten gold. The air shifts: more pond, less city.

"Let's go home," says Angelique. "Mama's gonna want us before dark."

"In a minute," says Jacob, reluctant to surrender the day.

"Last cast," Marcel agrees, but he's already winding in his line.

Alphonse stands, stretching. "One more try."

He finds a new spot, farther down the bank, where the mud is darker, almost blue-black. He squats, digging with the screwdriver, tongue poking from the corner of his mouth in concentration.

Jacob watches from a distance. "You're never gonna find anything," he says, but not loud enough for Alphonse to hear.

But Alphonse does find something. The screwdriver hits resistance, a dull metallic thunk, and he leans in, fingers scraping at the mud.

"Hey!" he yells. "I got something!"

The others converge, trampling the grass. Jacob gets there first, kneeling to inspect.

"It's just a pipe," says Marcel, but even he sounds unsure.

"No," says Angelique. "It's wood. Look."

She brushes away the top layer, revealing the edge of a weathered plank, stained dark and shot through with streaks of red clay. The wood is splintered at one end, as if broken by force. Jacob tests the exposed bit, fingers probing for weakness. The plank gives, just slightly, then stops.

"It's stuck on something," he says. "Help me."

The four of them dig, hands and tools and sticks, prying loose the earth around the object. The effort is messy, the mud sucking at their arms, but together they uncover the shape—a box, or a chest, its sides eaten by rot and the hardware pitted with rust. A hinge is visible, the metal so corroded it flakes away at the touch. The top is blackened, scorched at one corner as if kissed by fire.

For a long moment, no one speaks. The world is just the four of them and the thing they've found, half in and half out of the ground.

"What is it?" whispers Angelique, but she knows, or thinks she knows.

Jacob is first to act. He wedges his hands beneath the lip and pulls, straining until the box shifts free with a wet sucking sound. The weight is heavier than it looks, but he manages to wrestle it onto the shore, where the others can examine it.

Marcel runs a hand along the top. "It's locked."

"Not really," says Alphonse. "The lock's busted." He pokes a finger through the hole, wiggling it.

"Let's open it," says Angelique, her voice barely above a whisper.

Jacob hesitates, then nods. "On three."

They count together, breathless and dirty, and on three, Jacob lifts the lid.

Inside, darkness and the smell of old smoke. The box is lined with cloth, or what's left of it, and underneath, shapes that glint in the dying light.

None of them speak. They just stare, and in the silence, the lake reflects their faces—astonished, greedy, afraid—four shadows caught in the act of becoming something else.

For a long, dry minute, no one moves. The four siblings crouch tight as a nest of field mice, breath shallow, faces half-lit by the spill of evening over the bank. The box sits between them like a small, sullen guest, the scent of scorched cloth and mildew knifing through the usual pond stench. Jacob is first to act, pushing his hand into the gap and fumbling the slick, rotten lining.

Angelique leans over his shoulder, sharp-eyed and ready to pounce. "Careful. You'll break it."

"I'm not gonna break anything." Jacob peels back a layer of charred felt, revealing the guts of the chest: stacks and stacks of paper, each bundle wrapped with a blue band. The first is little more than mulch, but beneath, the bills—wet, but legible—fan out in green and gray and the strange, unblinking faces of old money.

"Is that real?" Marcel asks, voice a little hoarse. He reaches in, lifts a single note, turns it over, studies the watermark. The ink has run in spots, the portrait blurring into something almost kind.

"It's real," says Angelique, but she sounds as if she wishes it weren't.

Alphonse is quiet, sitting back on his heels, eyes flicking between the chest and his siblings. "How much is there?" he asks, but not to anyone in particular.

Jacob starts counting, stacking each bill with a care learned from watching Beth pay rent, counting once, then twice, then again for insurance. He stops at twenty, looks up, then down at the rest. "There's a lot. Maybe a thousand? More?"

Marcel's eyes go round. "We're rich," he says, but it comes out small, as if the words are too big for his mouth.

Angelique takes a handful, flicks through it, then pinches her lips shut. "They are soaked," she says. "Half of this is ruined. Look."

Jacob shrugs. "The other half is good."

"It's not ours," Angelique says. "Somebody's missing this."

"It's in the ground. It's nobody's now." Marcel closes the lid, sits on it. "We found it. That's what matters."

"Maybe it belonged to a bank robber," says Alphonse, grinning. "Maybe he hid it here before he got caught."

"Or before he died," Angelique adds, not unkind. "That's why no one came for it."

Jacob looks at her, then at the box. His hand trembles as he closes it, an involuntary spasm. "We should take it home."

Marcel's foot bounces against the dirt. "We can't just carry it through the street. Someone'll see."

"Who cares?" Alphonse says. "They'll just think it's junk."

Angelique hesitates. "What if Mama finds out?"

"She won't," Jacob says, but his voice is less certain than before. "We'll hide it in the shed, wait until we can figure it out."

A silence falls, each child trapped in the math of what comes next.

The walk home seems longer than the walk there. The chest is heavier now, as if it's absorbed all the doubt and worry they cannot say aloud. Jacob carries the bulk, Marcel taking one end, Alphonse walking ahead with a stick as if clearing a path through invisible enemies. Angelique follows behind, scanning the sidewalks for witnesses, her own heart beating time against her ribs.

They make it to the house without incident. The shed, half-collapsed and smelling of rust, welcomes their secret with a groan. Jacob stows the box behind the crates, layering old tarps and the carcass of a broken radio over it. He wipes his hands on his jeans, then stands back, admiring his own caution.

Inside, the kitchen is warm, the table crowded with bowls of macaroni and the promise of canned peaches for dessert. Beth is busy at the stove, her hair wrapped and her sleeves rolled high. She looks up as they enter, eyes narrowing. "Why are you so dirty?"

Jacob answers first, "We were at the lake."

Marcel chimes in, "We caught a frog."

Alphonse shrugs, "Didn't catch any fish, though."

Beth grunts, unconvinced. "Take off those shoes before you come in here. I'm not scraping mud off the floor all night."

They obey, each peeling off a layer of the day and lining it up by the door. Angelique lingers, watching Beth for any sign that their secret has followed them inside. But Beth is occupied, already thinking of tomorrow's chores.

At the table, they eat fast, heads down, barely tasting the food. The chest in the shed pulses at the edge of every conversation, a silent guest no one dares mention.

After dinner, Jacob slips outside, checks the shed, then circles the house twice, making sure the chest is safe. He returns to his room, lies on the cot, stares at the ceiling.

He thinks about the money—the way it looked, the way it felt —and wonders if things would be better if they kept it, if they bought new shoes, new clothes, maybe even a color TV like the neighbors. He imagines the possibilities, then pushes them away.

In the other room, Marcel talks in his sleep. Angelique whispers a prayer. Alphonse counts backward from one hundred, eyes open in the dark, as if calculating how long it will take for the world to change.

The next morning, Jacob wakes early. He waits for the rest of the house to come alive, then pulls Angelique aside in the hallway.

"We have to tell someone," he says, voice urgent. "We can't just keep it. If we get caught, we're dead."

Angelique studies him, then nods. "We go to the police. Say we found it. Maybe they'll give us a reward."

Jacob smiles, relieved. "You're smart."

"Smarter than you, anyway." She smirks, but the tension in her shoulders is gone.

They gather the others, tell them the plan. Marcel protests, wants to keep the money, but Angelique talks him down. "It's not ours," she says. "It never was."

Alphonse is quiet, but when the time comes, he helps carry the chest, steady and sure as ever.

The sky is the color of boiled milk as the four of them shuffle through the doors of the Emeryville police station, a chest—dirt-streaked, charred, patched with tape—cradled between Jacob and Marcel. They step onto the worn linoleum, the weight of the box sagging their arms, the memory of what they almost kept buzzing behind their eyes.

The lobby is mostly empty, save for a man in a battered suit who glances up from his newspaper and a secretary behind glass, filing her nails with the slow determination of someone paid by the hour. Fluorescent tubes flicker overhead, lending every surface an unnatural pallor; even Angelique's brown skin takes on a ghostly cast, and the hollows under Alphonse's eyes become canyons.

Jacob approaches the counter, chest clutched to his ribs, and waits. After a moment, the secretary looks up, inspects them in the way of someone used to children carrying trouble.

"We found this," Jacob says, voice dry from the heat and nerves. He sets the box down on the counter, its arrival punctuated by a dull thud.

The woman stands, leans in, and lifts the lid with a pencil. She stares a long beat at the nest of bills, then at the children, then again at the box. "You didn't steal this, did you?"

"No, ma'am," says Jacob. "We dug it up at the lake."

She raises an eyebrow, then calls out, "Sergeant Mason! I need you up here."

A heavyset man in a blue shirt arrives, hands in pockets, his gait slow but sure. He listens as Jacob repeats the story: the fishing trip, the worms, the scrape of screwdriver on metal. The man lets out a low whistle as he flips through the soggy, ripped bills. "Well, I'll be damned," he says, not unkindly. "It's a treasure chest, all right. Where'd you say you found it?"

"Buried at the north bank," says Angelique, voice flat. "Near the old tire swing."

The sergeant considers this, then gestures them to a bench. "Sit tight. You might be here a while."

Time slows inside the station. The tick of the wall clock becomes a metronome. Secretaries answer phones, then hang up. People come in, file reports, leave. No one pays the children much attention. Jacob sits with arms folded, feet planted wide; Marcel cracks his knuckles, then chews at a hangnail until it bleeds. Angelique picks at a thread on her sleeve, her eyes never leaving the box. Alphonse reads the pamphlets stacked on the table— Missing, Wanted, Lost—until he knows them by heart.

After an hour, a detective in a wrinkled brown suit appears. He greets them by name, one at a time, as if he's memorized a list. "I'm Detective Lawson," he says, smiling with only half his face. "Let's see what you've brought me."

He carries the box to a back room and motions them to follow. Inside, under brighter lights and the stink of old coffee, he begins to pull the money out, laying it flat across a blotter, counting aloud as he goes. "One... two... three... four..." He stops at fifty, then stacks the rest into soggy towers.

"Most of these are ruined," he says. "But there's enough here to make a difference."

Angelique frowns. "What do you mean?"

Lawson leans back, steeples his fingers. "You ever hear of the Emeryville Bandit?" The kids shake their heads. "Back in the forties, fella named Earl Stokes robbed banks from here to Richmond. Never got caught. Last job, he took two grand and vanished. People said he drowned in the lake, but nobody ever found the money. Guess we know where it ended up."

Marcel looks at Jacob, awe creeping into his voice. "We found a legend."

"You did," says Lawson. "And you did the right thing by bringing it in."

He takes down their names, writes a report, then leaves them waiting while he speaks to someone on the phone. When he returns, he holds a yellow envelope, thick and official.

"County policy is, you get ten percent of any recovered loot, if it's not claimed by next-of-kin. That's the law."

Jacob does the math. "A hundred dollars?"

Lawson grins, shakes his head. "Most of this is trashed, but there's a thousand here the bank can use. So you get a hundred."

The envelope feels weightless when Jacob takes it, but he senses the enormity of it—more money than he's ever held.

"Split it four ways," Lawson says, "or save it for something big. Up to you." He winks, then turns back to his paperwork.

They leave the station in a wedge, the envelope tucked under Jacob's arm. The sky outside has gone from milk to lead, clouds banking low. The walk home is silent at first. Each is busy with their own calculations: Jacob picturing Beth's face when he gives her the news, Marcel already spending his quarter-share on new sneakers and a transistor radio, Angelique wondering if a hundred dollars could really buy her a week's peace from the world, Alphonse thinking—always, always thinking—about what they could have done with the whole chest.

At the corner, Jacob stops, looks at the others. "We tell Mama everything?"

Angelique nods, firm. "Of course. It's not a secret."

Marcel shrugs. "She won't believe it."

Alphonse just smiles, a small, sly twist of the lips. "She'll believe."

They walk the last few blocks in step, the envelope growing heavier with each footfall. It is not the money that weighs most, but the knowledge of what might have been—the unclaimed life, the choices left buried at the bottom of the lake.

At the door, they pause, exchange glances. Jacob lifts his chin. "Let's go."

They step inside, four shadows, a hundred dollars, and a story nobody in the world can take from them.

Beth was at the stove, the sharp scent of onions and smoke rising as she stirred a pot of beans, when the children tumbled in, faces flushed from the sun and something else—some secret brightness she hadn't seen in a long time. Jacob hung back, hands shoved deep in his pockets, while Marcel lingered by the door. Angelique stepped forward, eyes shining, Alphonse at her side, mouth pressed tight.

"Mama," Angelique said, holding out an envelope. "We got something for you."

Beth wiped her hands on her apron, suspicion knitting her brow. "What's this now?"

Jacob nudged Angelique, who handed over the envelope. Beth opened it slowly, expecting a school note or another bill, but what slid out was a crisp ten-dollar bill—then another, and another, until ten lined the kitchen table, neat as Sunday gloves.

"Where did this come from?" Beth's voice was sharp, warning. "You better not have stolen—"

"We found it, Mama," Marcel blurted, "by the lake—buried, like treasure. We gave it to the police. They said it was from some old story, a bank robber or something, and let us keep part of it."

Angelique nodded. "Detective Lawson said we did the right thing."

Beth stared at the money, then at each of her children, searching for any sign of deceit. All she found was pride, mingled with nervous hope.

She exhaled, slow and shaky. "Lord have mercy," she said, voice softening. "You did right?"

Jacob nodded. "We did, Mama."

Beth gathered the bills and pressed them flat, her hands trembling. "We'll use this for something good," she said, eyes misting. "You hear me? Food, shoes, maybe a little put away. You children… you done right."

For a moment, the kitchen was silent except for the bubbling beans, the children standing a little taller, the world—if only for a breath—tilted toward grace.

CHAPTER 8

Wilbur sat alone on the warped wooden porch. The house was finally finished. dusk settling softly over Emeryville like a threadbare purple blanket. The day's labor clung to him—limestone grit beneath his cracked fingernails, a deep soreness radiating through his broad shoulders, the persistent ache of dreams deferred throbbing in his temples. He watched the last copper rays of sunlight catch on the peeling robin's-egg blue window trim he'd painted himself three summers ago, the modest clapboard house a patchwork testament to every odd job he'd picked up since arriving in California with next to nothing. He thought about the General Motors assembly line—the endless metallic clank of chassis parts being fitted together, the red-faced floor supervisor's oil-stained clipboard slapping against his thigh as he barked orders, the way each twelve-hour shift left him hollowed out like a stripped engine block, longing for something substantial he couldn't name but felt in his marrow.

Inside, Beth's honeyed contralto voice drifted through the rusted screen door, corralling the children with practiced patience, her evening prayers rising and falling like the Gulf tide he still sometimes dreamed about. Wilbur closed his heavy-lidded eyes, letting her familiar words wash over him like baptismal water. He remembered, suddenly, the cool weight of wet mortar in his calloused hands back in Arkansas, the steady hypnotic rhythm of trowel scraping against rough brick, the quiet soul-deep satisfaction of building something solid meant to outlast the frailty of flesh.

He looked at his hands—callused, battered, yet steady enough to hold a trowel without trembling. He flexed his fingers, remembering how they'd once smoothed mortar between bricks with the same care Beth used when braiding Angelique's hair. A vision flickered: himself standing before a foundation he'd laid, his name scratched into the wet cement, still visible decades after his timecard had been punched for the last time. His chest expanded with a warmth that rivaled the sunset bleeding across the Emeryville sky.

That evening, as the children settled and Beth finished the last of the dishes, Wilbur sat at the kitchen table, turning his thoughts over out loud. "Beth," he began, voice careful, "I been thinking on learning a trade. Masonry. It'd bring in more money, give us something solid."

Beth paused, plate in hand, eyes searching his face. "You always did have a steady hand," she said softly, then set the dish down with a sharp clink. "But we came all this way for something better, not just different."
He nodded, then looked away. "I want to leave something behind. Build up, not just get by. But Lord knows I'm scared too, Beth.""

Wilbur's first day as a brick mason dawned cold and bright, the sky a hard blue over the construction site on the edge of Emeryville. The foreman tossed him a battered trowel and pointed to a pallet of red bricks, skepticism plain in his eyes. Wilbur just nodded, rolling up his sleeves, feeling the weight of possibility settle into his bones.

The work came back to him like a hymn remembered—mixing mortar to just the right consistency, laying each brick so it fit snug, tapping it true with the heel of his hand. At first, the other men watched in silence, waiting for the ageing Southern newcomer to falter. But Wilbur's line was straight, his corners sharp, and he never paused to rest, even when sweat stung his eyes.

By the end of the week, the foreman clapped him on the back. "You got good hands, King. Not many could finish that wall in a day." Wilbur grinned, pride warming him from the inside out.

With each new job, his confidence grew. He learned to read blueprints, to calculate just how many bricks each foundation demanded. The city changed beneath his hands: patios bloomed behind simple houses, storefronts rose square and sturdy along the avenue. Wilbur's reputation followed him—quiet, steady, fair with his prices and careful with his craft.

At home, he brought back extra pay, the first real comfort the family had known. Beth marveled when he came in evenings with his jeans caked in gray dust, the children rushing to greet him. "Built that new storefront on San Pablo today," he'd say, holding his back with pride and exhaustion. "They said it'll stand longer than we will."

On Sundays, he'd walk past buildings he'd helped raise, running his finger along the mortar, knowing every seam by sight and feel. In each wall, he saw more than just labor—he saw proof that a man could shape something lasting, something good, out of sweat and hope and steady hands.

One evening, after a long day laying the foundation for a neighbor's new porch, Wilbur lingered out by the garage, hands raw and dusted with mortar. He gazed at the sturdy lines of his own house—the blue window trim, the brickwork solid beneath the surface paint. For the first time, he allowed himself to wonder if what he built with his hands might echo something deeper, something spiritual.

As twilight bled into night, Wilbur heard Beth leading the

children in prayer. The cadence of her voice reminded him of the slow, careful rhythm of placing brick atop brick, each word a small weight, each pause a gap filled with hope. The urge to build out beyond the walls of his home stirred inside him—a longing to do more than provide, to leave something lasting in the hearts of his community.

That Sunday, as he walked past the buildings he'd helped raise, Wilbur traced his calloused fingertips over the rough-hewn brickwork. He knew every seam by sight and feel—the hairline crack running beneath the drugstore window, the slightly uneven mortar line on the corner of Mrs. Johnson's porch, the perfect symmetry of the bank's eastern wall. He thought of his neighbors, their burdens and sorrows tucked inside walls no one else bothered to patch—like old man Garvey's leaking basement that flooded each spring, or the widow Simmons' chimney that whistled mournfully during winter storms. That knowing, that tending, felt holy as communion wine on his tongue.

When the old pastor's voice faltered days later—breaking mid-sermon like a dry twig underfoot—Wilbur understood, with a certainty as sure as a plumb line, that laying foundations was his gift. The weight of the congregation's worried glances pressed against his shoulders as heavily as a wheelbarrow full of wet cement. Whether with mortar or with prayer, he could shape something that would hold through storm and time. The tools in his trunk—the trowel with its worn wooden handle, the level with its perfect bubble of air, the square with its right angles —and the gospel in his mouth belonged, somehow, to the same calling.

One foggy Sunday morning, at Triumph Church, where the wooden pews creaked like old bones and stained glass filtered the light into jewel-toned puddles on the floor, the congregation gathered restless in the sanctuary. The old pastor's voice cracked as he announced his departure, each syllable brittle as communion wafer, his liver-spotted hands trembling against the pulpit's edge. Wilbur's hand gripped the pew until his knuckles ached white as bleached cotton. He rose halfway, the wood groaning beneath him, sat back down, then finally stood, mouth dry as Arkansas dust in August. "We need a shepherd," he said, the words catching in his throat like fish bones. "Someone to hold us together." His gaze drifted to the exit door with its peeling green paint and loose brass handle. "If you'll have me, I'll serve."

Beth's fingers twisted her handkerchief into a tight coil, the embroidered edges disappearing into her dark fist. Her eyes found his across the sea of bowed heads—not quite pride, not quite worry, but something more challenging to name, like the color of the sky just before a storm breaks.

When the elders laid hands on Wilbur, their prayers felt like stones being stacked upon his shoulders—smooth river rocks, jagged granite, heavy limestone—each word adding weight. That night, he stood in the unfinished house he'd built, running his palm over the garage wall where mortar still cured, soft enough to take his fingerprint, leaving a whorled impression like a signature. Two paths stretched before him now—the trowel and the pulpit.

CHAPTER 9

At Kennedy Elementary, the ceilings arched up with impossible optimism, the floors a checkerboard of mud and anxiety, everything painted in that particular shade of institutional yellow that managed to bleach the faces of teachers and children alike. On the King children's first day, the noise in the hall was a living organism—squeals ricocheting, desks scraping, the stampede of sneakers and the ozone tang of disinfectant. The building itself seemed to pulse with a nervous energy, as if the walls braced for impact from the endless collisions of childhood.

Jacob led the pack, angular and solemn in his hand-me-down corduroy slacks, eyes already scanning for threat or opportunity. Marcel trailed close, mouth set in the hard line of a boy who'd memorized every slight. Angelique, pressed and pressed again by Beth that morning until her hair and dress were nearly military, glided in with her brothers' shadows flanking her.

There was no easing into this world—the first bell had barely faded before the storm broke.

Their first classroom was a split-level battlefield. The teachers, bright-eyed and iron-spined, delivered rules in starched sentences and sharp glances. The King children, not yet wise enough to hide their accent or the poverty sewn into their seams, absorbed every instruction with a blend of earnestness and skepticism. In Arkansas, school had meant knowing your place—Blacks in one rotting bungalow, Whites in another, the border clear and enforced by generations of habit. The biggest difference here was that the boundaries were invisible, but just as real. Clusters of Black, Filipino, Chinese, and Mexican kids orbited each other in wary orbits, English the only lingua franca but shaped and accented by a dozen different histories.

The first lunch period was a crash course in social topography. The cafeteria, with its bolted-down tables and impossible din, ran on fierce loyalty and territorial claims. The Kings ended up at the periphery, perched like newgrown crows on a wire, watching the careful choreography of the other kids. Lunches unwrapped: Jacob's bologna sandwich and apple, Angelique's two hard-boiled eggs, Marcel's peanut butter crackers crammed into a paper towel.

The insults started slow but built up like floodwater behind a dam. "Country boy," a boy snorted as Jacob passed. "You ride a tractor to school?" hissed a girl at Angelique, who willed herself not to flinch. Marcel, who already dreamed in the language of fists, cataloged every jibe and sneer, compiling a list of enemies. After the first week, even the school nurse knew the King children by name, summoned for bloody noses, black eyes, or the taut, silent visits that meant something was festering deep but unseen.

Beth tried to arm them. Every morning was a ritual: face the bathroom mirror, tie the shoes, recite the lines. "You are a King, and you are smart." "You are a King, and you are strong." But by week three, even Beth's mantras had lost their magic. Jacob started coming home later and later, claiming "he was at the library" when he'd clearly been nowhere near a book. Marcel grew sullen, refusing to talk about his days, eyes going flat and wild at the first hint of interrogation. Angelique began to mimic the voices of her tormentors at the dinner table, trading her drawl for a hard Northern sharpness, trying it on for size.

The old patterns didn't fit anymore. Back in Texarkana, church and family had been the whole of their social world, boundaries policed by Beth's switch and Wilbur's sermons. Here, the city bled into everything, turning even the safest routines inside out. On Sundays, the King family would dress in their best—Wilbur in his only suit, Beth's hat rivaling the white-lace angels on the altar—and troop to the Triumph Church. The congregation greeted them with practiced smiles, but even there the divisions crept in. The original families, descended from the beaming pioneers in the church's faded photographs, eyed the newcomers with a mix of suspicion and condescension. The Kings sat in their assigned pew like a row of chess pieces, shifting uneasily as the preacher thundered about the dangers of worldliness and pride.

At home, the King children learned to adapt along the seams. Jacob discovered that a carefully timed joke could diffuse a hallway confrontation; he learned too that fighting back, when absolutely necessary, earned a respect that sometimes outlasted the bruises. Marcel became notorious for his pranks —once convincing a substitute teacher that the fire alarm was scheduled for every Tuesday at exactly 2:17. Angelique, ever the meticulous observer, cracked the code of the school's elaborate social ladder. She realized that the Filipino girls with the perfect hair and the gold hoop earrings sometimes let her sit at their bench if she complimented their shoes. She also learned that no matter how well she stripped her voice of the South, it would always sound foreign to someone.

Miss Alderman's voice crackled through the receiver for the third time that week. "Mrs. King? We need to discuss Marcel's behavior." Beth gripped the phone cord tight, twisting it around her finger until the tip went white. The same script followed —Jacob's failing math, Angelique's "attitude," Alphonse's tears. Each time, Beth murmured the same promises into the plastic mouthpiece, her voice steady even as her free hand clenched. Later, with moonlight slanting across the worn floorboards, she pressed her forehead to clasped hands beside her bed. "Lord," she whispered, "give me strength to guide them through this wilderness." The prayer hung in the darkness, unanswered but necessary, like breath itself.

Alphonse, who was still too young to carry the armor of sarcasm or bravado, suffered most acutely. He cried the first time a teacher mispronounced his name, turning it into something ridiculous and foreign. He cried again when two older boys cornered him behind the gym, called him "Al-fawn-see" and made him eat a handful of playground woodchips. His siblings tried to coach him. "Don't let them see you cry," whispered Marcel, but Alphonse couldn't help it. He missed everything from the old world: the familiar drawl, the safe rituals, the feeling of being known and named and not just another body in the crowd.

There were bright spots, tiny and fierce. An afternoon when Jacob scored the winning basket during recess and for a fleeting moment, the rest of the school chanted his name, the syllables sweet and clean. A day Angelique's essay on "The Person I Admire Most" was read aloud to the class, its lines about her mother's iron will and gentle hands earning her a gold star and a rare, genuine smile from her teacher. The time Marcel, caught mid-fight with a seventh grader twice his size, managed to talk his way out of the principal's office with a story so convoluted and charming that the principal laughed and let him off with a warning.

But the cost was ever-present. Every adaptation, every tiny victory, carried a shadow price. Jacob started to wear his hair different, then his clothes, then his entire posture. Soon he moved like a city kid, all casual slouch and wary, narrowed eyes. Marcel's jokes grew sharper, crueler, sometimes aimed at his own siblings just to keep ahead of the curve. Angelique, who once recited Bible verses from memory, now practiced cursing in the mirror, soft at first and then louder, until even Beth had to admit that her daughter sounded more like an Oakland teenager than a Southern belle.

Home never felt quite right after that. The blue-trimmed house, always noisy and cluttered, began to tremble with new tensions. Rage simmered under every meal; plates sometimes slammed onto the table, words sometimes broken mid-sentence by a sudden, stifled sob. Wilbur retreated into late-night Bible study, the pages illuminated by a single lamp, his shadow hunched and unmoving. Beth doubled down on discipline, enforcing earlier curfews and zero tolerance for backtalk, but even she sensed the edge slipping from her commands.

The children huddled together at night, sometimes in the boys' room, sometimes on the back stoop, each trying to explain the world outside in terms the others could bear. Jacob would invent stories about the teachers, giving them secret lives and wild adventures; Marcel would embellish every insult until it became farce, and the others laughed even when it hurt. Angelique wrote her own name over and over in her notebook, shaping the letters until she almost believed they belonged to someone else. Alphonse, restless and small, would lie on the carpet and listen, eyes wide, clinging to every strange new word and story.

They learned, slowly, the art of camouflage. How to blend in when necessary, how to stand out when it counted. By the end of the first year, the Kings had mapped the veins and arteries of the school, knew which teachers would look the other way and which ones would call home at the first sign of trouble. They could spot the kids who would fight, the ones who would run, the ones who would hide. They learned what jokes were safe and what jokes could get you jumped after school. They learned how to take a hit and not cry. They learned how to pretend.

By June, the smell of the school had seeped into their skin. Bleach and wax, dried milk sour in the cracks between tiles, the dank undertone of gym mats sweating in the dark somewhere behind the cafeteria. They wore it home on their clothes and in their hair, a badge of having survived the day.

Jacob stopped flinching at the insults. He rolled them around in his mouth, spat them back when it served him, or chewed them until all that was left was the quiet certainty that nobody had to like you for you to walk the hall without fear. He'd learned the rhythm of the place: the lull before the morning bell, the mad surge at lunch, the way everything sharpened in the hour before last period.

Marcel fed on the chaos. He prowled, sniffing out the soft spots, figured out quick that if you could make them laugh, you could make them leave you alone. But the laughter had to sting. His pranks grew more surgical, his jokes edged in cruelty that felt lighter than getting bruised. He would plot all morning, arms folded, nail the punchline at lunch, and ride the infamy through the afternoon.

Angelique haunted the periphery. She watched how the popular girls linked arms and whispered, how the teachers' favorite sat up front and never let their hair out of place. She practiced that stillness, the silences between sentences. In class, she raised her hand with the right amount of hesitation; in the halls, she matched her step to the tempo of the crowd. She changed her voice, changed her walk, changed her laugh. At home, when Beth tried to press her back into the shape of herself, Angelique just blinked, slow and deliberate, and moved on.

Isaiah mastered invisibility, mastered the art of not catching the teacher's eye. He let the days pass over him, ducked the worst of it, memorized the safe routes between classrooms. At lunch, he rationed out crackers and swapped stories about the animals they'd known back in Arkansas, stories so unlikely even Marcel left them alone.

Alphonse flailed to adapt. He tried to mimic the others, but every mask slipped. He said the wrong thing, or said nothing when he should have spoken. He came home with his collar ripped or his backpack inside out, and some days, with a bruise he insisted was from a game, not a fight. The laughter hurt worst —the reedy, high-pitched sound that told you exactly where you stood. Some days, Angelique would find him hiding under the slide or pressed into the farthest corner of the yard, his face set in the determination of someone who had run out of good options.

In a place built on invisible borders and constant noise, the children of the King family learned to survive gradually— blending in with borrowed habits, shaped by the pressures of a city that never softened to welcome them. Day after day, they came home with the grit of Kennedy Elementary ingrained in their skin, each lesson in belonging paid for with a small act of surrender. They became experts at going unnoticed, or standing just enough apart to avoid being trampled, their accents toned down and laughter sharpened, their hopes sewn tight beneath thrift-store seams. The old rules no longer applied, but in finding new ways to endure, they built a kind of resilience— a cautious strength that would serve them in a world where fitting in was never guaranteed, and survival was its own quiet victory.

CHAPTER 10

Ten years came and went, seasons blending like watercolors on wet paper. The children grew like saplings—Jacob, the eldest, with a voice almost as deep as his father's; Marcel, quick and restless, never far from trouble; Angelique, sharp-eyed and watchful, always reading the room; Isaiah, quieter than the others, slipping into rooms unheard; Jeanne, brisk and orderly, forever straightening what her brothers left askew; Constance, wide-eyed and serious, content to observe from her quiet corner; Theresa, always scribbling poems in her notebook; and Armand, witty and charming; and Alphonse, tender-hearted and always trailing after his older siblings, hungry for their attention. Soon, the house brimmed with thunderous footfalls and bell-like laughter, each child's voice adding a new note to the family's chorus.

The Triumph Church had never lived up to its name, really, but some years it could fake it better than others. At mid-morning, the line of battered sedans and rusting station wagons snaked down the curb, their tailpipes breathing fog into the street. The familiar blue door, once so proud, now hung at a subtle diagonal —Wilbur had patched the hinges himself, but the years would not be bullied into submission.The church was a small square of brick hunkered tight in a grid of blacktop and chain-link fencing —the only building on the block still upright, its stained glass windows too thick for the gangs' stones to shatter, its blue paint scuffed but intact. On most days, it looked like a hazard beacon, a last warning for the world to steer clear. But on Sunday, the neighborhood woke up for it: women in hats and gloves, old men in shiny shoes limping up the walk with heads high and stories already stacking up behind their teeth. Even when fog strangled the sun, the place glowed—somehow holding off the rot cutting in from every side.

Wilbur stood near the entryway, watching Beth marshal the children through the crowds. He felt the eyes of the congregation: some proud, some skeptical, some measuring the stretch of his collar or the shine off his scalp. Ten years, and still some never called him "Pastor" without a raised eyebrow or hint of challenge in the bend of their lips. To them, he would always be Wilbur, the Colored man who built houses with his own hands and left the factory only to stand in front of a different assembly— this time a row of expectant faces, each waiting for him to fix what the world had broken.

The sanctuary was humid with anticipation, the scent of mothballs and hair oil clinging to the wooden beams so dense you could taste it. Wilbur squeezed past the front pew, his heart running fast, the sermon in his jacket pocket soft with revision and worry. The old pulpit, gouged by a generation of trembling hands, stood like a relic from a war nobody remembered winning. He spread his notes on the splintered top, smoothed his palm over the first page, and tried to ignore the tremor in his gut.

The pews filled in. A tide of restless children fidgeted and poked, their mothers flattening collars and hushing their complaints with a grip to the knee or a look. Wilbur's own brood scattered to the middle row—Jacob already prodding Marcel with his elbow, Angelique picking at her braids, Alphonse tucked between them like a question mark in a crowd of exclamation points.

Beth took up her post behind the choir, folding her hands with the air of a woman who dared someone to judge the set of her hat or the color of her stockings. Wilbur caught her eye for a split second before she turned, but it was enough: her approval landed on his shoulder like a steady weight, heavier and truer than anything the congregation could muster.

He cleared his throat, and the room flicked instantly to silence. Even the toddlers stilled, breath held, as if waiting for the punchline to a joke they'd already heard from their parents.

"Brothers and sisters," he says, letting the vowels stretch, holding the room in the slow, tensile grip of a practiced preacher, "today's message is on the trial of faith in a world that would see it broken."

He opens the Bible. His hands still bear the memory of trowels, the ridged calluses catching on the thin pages. He reads the passage from the Epistle of James—faith without works is dead—and as he speaks, the words gather heat. He can feel the room's breath change, the slight shifting of weight as the story comes alive.

He tells them about the orchards in Arkansas, the hard-won crop, the way the sun scorched both the faithful and the sinner with equal ferocity. He tells them about the day the well went dry, and how the entire town lined up at the river with buckets, the Black families on one side, the whites on the other, but thirst making kin of them all for one holy hour. He draws the line —subtle, invisible—between the world that was and the world they now inhabit, but the message is the same: only by suffering the heat do you know the sweetness of rain.

In the front row, Beth's face is unreadable, but her chin lifts half an inch at the right phrases. The children's attention drifts, as expected. Jacob tries to sneak a glance at the clock above the vestibule, but Angelique blocks his view with the edge of her hymnal, lips curled in a secret smile. Alphonse doodles in the margin of the bulletin, the pencil stolen from the Sunday school basket, and every now and then looks up, eyes as dark and bottomless as the lake.

Wilbur feels the sermon cresting—this is the part that matters. He slows his speech, draws the air down into his chest, and lets silence fill the cracks.

"In this life," he says, "you will find the path forked: one way easy, wide, paved with the promises of men; the other narrow, rough, and lined with sharp stones. The first leads to comfort, yes, but the second—ah, that second—is the way of the cross. Every brick laid, every meal made, every kindness given is a testimony not to our strength but to our endurance."

He closes the book. There is a hush, deep and unbroken, as if the congregation waits for permission to breathe again. He does not give it. Instead, he looks straight at the children, letting his gaze rest on each one in turn, measuring their future against the weight of his words.

"Let us pray."

Beth's fingers strike the first chord on the piano, and the sanctuary fills with "Hold On, Just a Little While Longer." Mrs. Jefferson's hand shoots up before the first verse ends, palm open to heaven. Deacon Williams rocks forward on arthritic knees, eyes squeezed shut. Wilbur's voice breaks through on the refrain —"Hold on"—so deep it vibrates the floorboards beneath the pulpit. His shoulders rise with each breath. Jacob's lips barely move, one eye on the clock. Angelique sings every word, while Alphonse watches his mother's back stiffen when Marcel stops singing altogether, suddenly fascinated by a loose thread on his cuff.

When the last note dies, Beth stands first. She glides to the altar and begins the communion prep: placing the little cups of grape juice in precise rows, setting out the wafers with a surgeon's care. Wilbur steps down from the pulpit, shedding the robe in a quick motion, revealing the pressed white shirt beneath, sleeves rolled at the forearm. He moves among the parishioners, shaking hands, offering brief blessings, enduring the small talk with a patience born of years in the fields.

Most of the congregation are like them—recent arrivals, hungry for the structure of home in a place that feels assembled from the debris of other cities. A few old-timers linger at the back, eyes wary, always watching for the slip, the error that will betray the Kings as impostors. Wilbur greets each with the same level warmth, but he notes the hierarchy, the subtle arrangements of power and suspicion that run deeper here than any river back home.

Beth finishes the communion, wipes down the altar, and then collects the children with a glance. She shepherds them to the basement, where the Sunday school meets. Wilbur watches her go, thinking—as he always does—that she is the real preacher in this family, her sermons delivered not in words, but in the choreography of duty.

Downstairs, the children explode into motion, each one drawn to a different part of the room. Jacob and Marcel stake out the ping-pong table, their rivalry resuming instantly. Angelique gravitates to the corner where the teenage girls gossip, sliding into the circle with a practiced indifference. Alphonse stands at the window, looking out at the street, his breath clouding the glass.

Wilbur stays upstairs, sweeping the sanctuary with the broom left in the corner. The work is familiar, almost restful. As he moves, he studies the space: the cracks in the mortar, the hairline fractures in the glass, the way the morning light shifts across the altar as the sun moves from east to west. He thinks of the church in Arkansas—bare wood, tin roof, the smell of dust and sweat. This place, for all its faults, is a fortress by comparison. Still, he wonders how long it will hold.

He finishes the sweep, stacks the bulletins, straightens the hymnals in each pew. By the time he's done, the congregation has thinned, the parking lot outside already returning to its weekday emptiness. Beth waits at the door, the children clustered around her: Jacob with a fistful of candy from the church office, Marcel with a bandage on his knee, Angelique clutching a secret note scribbled on ruled paper, Alphonse quiet and unencumbered.

Wilbur steps out into the sun, the day bright and sharp. He locks the doors behind him, makes sure each child is accounted for, and sets off down the walk. The city hums in the distance—the traffic, the trains, the low drone of ships on the bay—but within this block, for one thin slice of time, there is only the family, the church, and the silent, accumulating weight of what must be endured.

They arrive home just past noon, shoes dusted with pollen and city grime. The house is set back from the street—a flat rectangle of cinderblock and vinyl, its lawn a patchwork of crabgrass and bare dirt. Wilbur built it himself, scavenging from construction sites, trading labor for lumber and patience for pipes. He painted the window trim blue, like the church doors, so it would be visible from the far end of the block. Beth did not approve of the color, but she did not object, either; it was one of the few arguments Wilbur won without a fight.

Inside, the air is warm, heavy with the sweetness of onions and the sharp note of boiling greens. The kitchen is a single aisle, tiled in yellow, every surface alive with the mess of making: two pots jostling for space on the stove, a skillet of chicken skin popping in lard, beans simmering in a pot older than the house itself. Beth moves with the certainty of one who knows every inch of her domain, hips and shoulders aligned to maximize efficiency. She cracks pepper with the heel of her hand, tosses a pinch of salt over her shoulder—always the left, for luck—and wipes sweat from her upper lip with the back of her wrist.

The children disperse on entering, each finding a refuge from the enforced proximity of church. Jacob and Marcel disappear to the backyard, where a basketball rim hangs askew from the garage. Angelique goes straight to her room, closes the door, and lets the silence accumulate. Alphonse lingers in the living room, absently plucking at the loose threads on the arm of the sofa. Wilbur stands in the hallway a moment, listening for the rhythm of the house—hears the dribble and thunk of the ball outside, the brief snatch of pop music leaking from Angelique's headphones, the clatter of pans in the kitchen. He lets it fill him before he moves.

He changes out of the black robe, folding it with care and laying it across the back of the bedroom chair. He hangs the white shirt, careful not to crease it, and puts on a t-shirt and blue jeans, the uniform of a man at rest. He spends a moment at the dresser, straightening the photos that line the top: the wedding portrait, Beth's face soft and young; the baptism of Jacob, water beads on his infant head; a picture of the Arkansas house, long since burned or bulldozed. He touches each frame in sequence, then leaves the room.

Beth calls for help setting the table. Angelique emerges first, rolling her eyes but taking the plates without protest. She arranges them in perfect compass points, aligning the forks and knives with military precision. Marcel brings out the glasses—mismatched, chipped at the lip—and lines them up along the edge of the table. Jacob wipes the surface with a dish towel, then slides into his chair and props his elbows on the edge, defiant and unrepentant.

There is no centerpiece, just the food: chicken fried to a copper finish, greens slicked with ham hock, beans thick as mortar, and cornbread golden and crumbling at the edges. Beth waits until everyone is seated, then sinks into her chair, hands folded in her lap.

Wilbur bows his head. His prayer is short, but heavy:

"Lord, we thank you for the hands that prepared this food,

for the work that brought it here, for the grace that keeps us together. Bless us and keep us, and let no trouble cross this table today. Amen."

They eat. Conversation at first is sparse, the only sound the scrape of fork on plate, the wet chew of collards. Beth serves the food in measured portions, never too much, always watching to see what goes untouched. She eats slow, eyes darting from child to child, gauging their moods by the speed and violence of their bites.

Wilbur tries to start a conversation, as he always does:

"Service went well today," he says. "The choir sounded strong."

Beth nods. "Sister Hawkins has a new grandbaby. She brought pictures."

Angelique picks at her beans, feigning disinterest.

Jacob asks, "Can we go to the lake after dinner?"

Beth's face tightens. "Why? You didn't bring your homework."

"It's Sunday," Jacob says. "There's nothing due."

Beth looks at Wilbur for support. He shrugs, then turns to Angelique. "You want to go, too?"

She shakes her head. "I'm meeting Simone downtown. She got a job at the jewelry counter in Capwell's, and she said I could watch her work if I want."

Beth bristles. "You don't need to be running around that part of town. Not with all that mess going on."

Angelique lifts her chin. "It's not like I'll be alone. Simone's mother is there, too. She said we could go for ice cream."

Wilbur senses the edge in Beth's voice, the thing she does when she's about to say no but waits for him to say it first. He meets Angelique's eyes, sees the flicker of hope there, and decides.

"You can go," he says, "but be back before dinner."

Angelique grins, then lowers her head, hiding the smile. Beth says nothing, but her fingers drum the table, the sound tight and anxious.

Jacob seizes the moment. "So I can go to the lake?"

"Take Marcel," Wilbur says. "Don't stay past sundown."

Jacob nods, triumphant. Marcel gives a rare smile, and even Alphonse looks up from his food, interested.

Beth clears her throat. "Don't bring that mud into my kitchen, you hear? And watch out for the bigger kids. Last time, you came home with a black eye."

Jacob rolls his eyes. "That was nothing."

Beth fixes him with a look that brooks no argument. "It better be nothing again."

They finish the meal in relative peace. Beth serves slices of canned peaches for dessert, and even as she does, she eyes the children, waiting for them to betray some flaw in her plan. When the last bite is gone, she gathers the plates, stacking them with the efficiency of someone who has done this a thousand times.

The children scatter, their voices rising as they argue over who gets the best pole, who gets to ride in front, who gets the last word. Angelique disappears to her room, already plotting her afternoon. Beth watches them go, arms folded across her chest.

Wilbur stays at the table, nursing the final bite of cornbread. He feels the divide opening, the space between parent and child, between the life he chose and the life they will want. He wonders, as he often does, if this is what faith is: watching the people you love drift away, and trusting that they will come back on their own.

He stands, carries the empty bowls to the kitchen, and kisses Beth's shoulder as she scrapes the plates. Her body relaxes, just slightly, and she leans into him for a second before shooing him away.

"Go on," she says. "Keep an eye on those boys."

He does. He stands at the window, watching as Jacob and Marcel race down the street, the two of them already out of reach but not yet out of sight. The world outside is bright, the sky clear, the air alive with the promise of something more.

He hopes it will be enough.

The light is already slanting hard when Jacob and Marcel make it to the lake. The water is low, silted green, banded at the margin with tire tracks and the carcasses of last year's reeds. They set the poles on the cracked concrete edge but do not bother to bait them. Marcel skips stones, his throws growing longer, more reckless, until one arcs so far it almost hits the canoe of a man trawling for carp in the middle distance.

They watch the boats, mostly: tinnies and rowboats, but also the slick fiberglass of pleasure craft, occasionally the flash of a sail from the yacht club on the other side of the embankment. Jacob points to the men smoking on the docks, the girls sunning themselves on the rocks, the clusters of college kids who lounge with radios and six-packs, their voices carrying on the wind like news from another universe.

"That'll be us," Jacob says, though he cannot say when.

Marcel shrugs. "It's just water."

But Jacob sees more: the city beyond, the web of bridges, the promise of other shores. He wonders how far he could get if he just started walking, no map, no plan—how long it would take before someone noticed he was gone.

They sit for a while in companionable quiet, their shadows growing longer and thinner. Marcel plucks at the line of his rod, a nervous habit, then says: "You ever think about leaving?"

Jacob does not answer right away. He kicks a stone into the water, watches the ripples erase the sky. "All the time," he says. "But we can't. Mama would kill us."

Marcel grins. "Maybe we bring her with us."

Jacob laughs. "She'd hate it. All that noise."

He means the city, but also the world, the future, everything waiting out there. He means the sound of traffic, the shriek of brakes, the sirens that cut the night in half.

Marcel says, "You ever wonder if Daddy gets tired? Of all this?"

Jacob considers. "He never lets on. But maybe he does."

Marcel is quiet, then: "You think he wants to go back?"

Jacob shakes his head. "He's not like that. He just wants us to be better than him."

They watch the sun drop behind the stack of the old cannery, the sky going from gold to gunmetal. Neither moves to reel in the lines, not even when it's clear the fish have no interest in biting. The city lights begin to come up, one window at a time, and in the distance, a ship's horn sounds, long and low.

Angelique and Alphonse take the shortcut past the old General Motors plant. The building is sealed now, its windows blacked by tar and dust, but even closed, it exerts a kind of gravity.

Alphonse runs his fingers along the chain link fence, the click and scrape echoing his steps. Angelique ignores the plant, scanning ahead for the first glimpse of the downtown strip—she can already see the glow of neon and hear the beat of music from the pinball arcade three blocks away.

They walk in silence, but their bodies communicate: Angelique sets the pace, quick and fluid, while Alphonse floats behind, a silent satellite. He is small for his age, hair cut close and face unreadable. She catches him staring at her sometimes, as if he is waiting for her to make a mistake.

They cross the avenue. A city bus hisses to a stop, its doors folding open, and a group of teenagers spills onto the sidewalk. They are beautiful, in the way of city kids—clothes bright and cut close, shoes spotless, voices loud but not cruel. One girl wears gold hoops the size of bracelets, her hair twisted into a gleaming crown. She laughs at something a boy says, her hand resting easy on his arm.

Angelique slows, drawn to their orbit. She feels the pulse of music leaking from their portable radio—new, sharp, nothing like the hymns at church—and for a moment, she imagines herself part of them, talking about nothing, daring the world to look away.

Alphonse tugs at her sleeve. "We should go," he says, voice low.

She lingers. The girl with the hoops meets her gaze, then gives a quick, appraising nod. Angelique nods back, but before she can say anything, Alphonse pulls harder. She lets herself be steered, but glances back at the cluster, memorizing the way they stood, the way they occupied space as if they owned it.

They continue to Capwell's, where Simone waits in her green uniform, face lit up by the display case. They wave through the glass, then settle on the bench outside, talking about school, about boys, about the possibility of working at Capwell's together someday. The talk is half real, half pretend, but it is enough.

When curfew nears, Angelique checks her watch and sighs. "We should head back."

Alphonse is already on his feet. "Daddy said before dinner."

They walk home in near-darkness, the streetlights flickering on as they pass. Angelique is quiet now, but her mind runs back to the bus stop, to the music, to the weightless way the girl moved through the world.

At home, Wilbur sits at the kitchen table, a yellow legal pad in front of him, the edges already curled from erasure and revision. He drafts next Sunday's sermon, but the words do not come easy. He writes and scratches out, writes and scratches out, trying to bridge the gap between the world inside and the one encroaching from every direction.

Beth is in the living room, needle and thread moving through the hem of Angelique's skirt. She does not look up as the children file in—she listens instead, counting the seconds between the slam of the door and the thump of shoes against the wall. She notes the time, the number of voices, the pattern of their coming and going.

She senses Wilbur behind her, hovering. "You're not fooling anyone," she says.

He smiles, not bothering to deny it. He sets the sermon aside and joins her on the couch.

"They're restless," she says, eyes on the stitch. "Jacob talks like he's already a man. Angelique—" she sighs, "Angelique wants the whole city."

Wilbur nods. "That's how we raised them. To want more."

Beth snorts. "You make it sound holy."

He shrugs. "Maybe it is."

She ties off the thread, bites the end, and smooths the fabric. "I just don't want them to get hurt. This city isn't what they think."

"It wasn't what we thought, either," Wilbur says. "But we learned."

She leans back, resting her head on his shoulder. For a moment, they say nothing.

"Do you miss it?" she asks. "The old place?"

He thinks. "Sometimes. But mostly I miss knowing who I was supposed to be."

Beth nods. "Me too."

They sit together, the house settling around them, the children's laughter filtering through the walls. Outside, the first siren of the evening wails, long and mournful, followed by another, and then another. The city is alive, always, never resting.

Wilbur closes his eyes, hears the echo of his own sermon: "Only by suffering the heat do you know the sweetness of rain."

The children's voices grow softer as the night deepens. In their rooms, they dream of water, of cities, of the weightless possibility of wanting more.

CHAPTER 11

The city bus is a cut-rate cathedral, sanctified by the stench of stale sweat, fryer oil, and adolescent deodorant, every aisle a narrow nave packed with supplicants in discount denim. Angelique King rides it home most days, chin tilted toward the little slip of sky visible through the bus's battered windows, thumb flicking absently at the page corners of her calculus book. She prefers the window seat, though she rarely looks out—no point, really, in cataloguing the same loop of billboards, liquor stores, and four-for-a-dollar taquerias. Still, today she keeps her face angled toward the glass, gaze stitched to the passing blur, a posture that signals her desire for distance as clearly as any sign hung around her neck.

It's standing-room only by the time they cross into Emeryville proper. The after-school crowd is thick today, a surge of bodies, backpacks, and restless energy. Angelique clocks them all: the coterie of varsity girls in matching hoodies and acrylic nails; the freshman boys, hunched and sullen, pretending not to notice the girls; the white-collar commuters up front, clutching briefcases like flotation devices. She registers every face, every voice, every new whiff of cigarette or cologne. Her brain has always worked this way—collect, sort, remember. It's the only thing she trusts.

The bus lurches to a halt at the stop near the new development, and that's when they get on: five of them, loud in every sense, shoulders squared and sneakers so clean they could slice a retina. The leader is a girl, tall, with a pink track suit and a gold chain thick as a jump rope. Two boys flank her—one in a red puffer jacket, the other in a windbreaker that looks like it costs more than Angelique's last two years of school supplies. They take up space like they own it, pushing through the crowd, demanding deference with elbows and glares.

"Man, this shit is deep," says the boy in the puffer, scanning for a seat. "Somebody better move."

No one moves. The girl laughs, high and sharp, then wades forward and wedges herself into the front-facing seat just ahead of Angelique. The boys spread out, taking the aisle and the steps by the rear door. Angelique lowers her eyes to her book, but does not read.

"Check this out," the girl says, digging into her coat pocket. She produces a roll of cash, fans it with her fingers. "Guess how much?"

The boy in the windbreaker leans over, voice pitched low. "You didn't."

"Bitch, I did! Four fifty, straight from the register. The poor guy didn't even blink."

"Y'all got no chill," says the puffer. "That's how you get caught."

The girl smirks. "We're not getting caught. Not unless you're the one snitching, which—I mean, look at you."

Angelique glances up through her lashes. The girl is older, maybe seventeen, with lashes for days and a mouth that telegraphs every mood before it's spoken. She laughs often, but the sound is controlled, as if she's measuring the effect. Her wrists are ringed with bangles, clinking with every gesture.

Behind her, the windbreaker boy cracks a joke about "making five hundred a drop." The group bursts into laughter, none of it friendly, all of it edged. They drop references Angelique has never heard: Red Chilie Peppers, the block on Sixty-Sixth, code names for people and places she files away for later. She listens, drawing the threads together, turning rumor into fact, impression into map.

The bus stops and starts, shuddering through traffic. The girl in the pink track suit angles her body toward Angelique, eyes raking her up and down. "You from around here?" she asks, loud enough for the entire row to hear.

Angelique does not answer immediately. She lets the question dangle, then looks up, expression flat. "Yeah."

"You look like you go to St. Columba," the girl says. "They all got that stuck-up face. What, you too good to talk?"

Angelique holds her gaze. "I just don't know you."

The girl tilts her head, considering. "Maybe you should."

Angelique gives a tiny shrug. "Maybe."

The bus rounds a corner hard, and the windbreaker boy nearly topples into the lap of a sleeping commuter. He laughs, recovers, then pulls a cell phone from his pocket and begins to tap out a message. The phone is new; the boy is not careful.

"Anyway," says the girl, turning back to her crew, "they're saying the next shipment is bigger. Like, big-big. We need more runners."

Puffer boy grunts. "You sure we can trust them?"

"Doesn't matter. They don't need to know anything. Just show up, deliver, get paid. That's it."

Angelique's spine straightens. She forces herself to turn the page of her calculus book, but her hands are too tight on the cover, and the sheet rips at the seam. She curses herself, wills her grip to slacken. She's been careful all her life, never to show her feelings, never to betray anything. But this—this feels like an audition, like the start of something she's been preparing for in the dark, waiting for her cue.

As the bus inches forward, the conversation keeps circling the same points: the money, the jobs, the ease of it all. Angelique listens for the details—where, when, who to call. She doesn't hear phone numbers, but she hears names: Peach, Tino, a guy called Uncle Red. She files them away.

Her stop is coming up, but she doesn't move. The girl in the track suit is watching her again, eyes sharp, lips pursed. Angelique meets the gaze, holding it a little longer this time.

"What's your name?" the girl demands.

"Angelique," she says, the word coming out clean and unadorned.

The girl grins. "I'm Jazzy. Remember me. I'll remember you."

Angelique nods, and that's the end of it.

The bus hisses to a halt. Angelique stands, swings her backpack over one shoulder, and slides past the trio, making sure to brush the pink track suit as she goes. The contact is intentional, but casual; she wants them to know she's not afraid.

Outside, the wind cuts through her jacket, and the sky is the color of wet cement. Angelique walks the half-mile home, every step replaying the conversation on the bus, every word and gesture combed for meaning. She moves fast, heart drumming, mind already plotting the angles.

Her house is small, set back from the street, a chain-link fence encircling the yard like a dare. She slips in the side door, kicks off her shoes, and drops her backpack on the kitchen table. No one is home yet—Beth works late at the church on Fridays, and Wilbur never returns from the site until well after dark.

Angelique sits at the table, spreads her books out, but does not open them. Instead, she stares at her own hands, the ink smudges on her knuckles, the bitten nails, the scar on her thumb from when she sliced it on a can of beans last year. These are the hands she will use to build the rest of her life. She is sure of it now.

She waits, listening to the silence, and wonders how long it will take before the city calls her back.

Angelique finds Alphonse behind the old cold storage plant, in the gap between the loading dock and the battered wall where delivery trucks used to dock, back when the city still imported more than it exported. He is waiting, as he always is—shoulders pressed to brick, hands jammed in his pockets, face hidden beneath the low brim of his cap. The spot is their church, the only place they can talk without the walls pressing in, without Beth's sharp ears or Wilbur's spectral presence infecting every word.

She comes in hot, pacing the broken concrete like a caged panther, breath already quickened from the walk. She can feel her heart in her throat, every pulse a reminder of the choice she's about to make.

Alphonse watches her without moving, eyes half-lidded. "What's the emergency?" he asks, but there's no real curiosity in it. He expects disaster; he is never disappointed.

She pulls up short, draws a deep breath, and says, "You want to make some real money?"

Alphonse lets out a small, sarcastic laugh. "What, you going to start selling your soul? I thought that was Dad's job."

She ignores it. "Listen," she says, and the command in her voice is enough to make him stand up straighter. "I'm not talking about a paper route, or minimum wage at the burger joint. I'm talking about five hundred dollars. Per drop."

Alphonse crosses his arms, rocks back on his heels. "Drop of what? Angelique, you don't even know what you're talking about."

She steps closer, close enough to smell the smoke on his collar, the secondhand reek of Lucky Strikes pilfered from the old man's stash. "I know exactly what I'm talking about. I heard it on the bus yesterday—the Red Chilie Peppers. They're recruiting. All you have to do is move a package, get paid, and no one asks questions."

He shakes his head. "You want to be a drug dealer? For real? You think Mom and Dad are going to be cool with that?"

Angelique rolls her eyes so hard she nearly loses her balance. "When was the last time you saw Mom buy anything besides clearance meat and off-brand cereal? Dad's busting his ass for pennies, and the only thing he brings home is concrete dust. You want to keep living like this?"

Alphonse shrugs. "It's not forever."

"That's what you said last year. And the year before that. You think college is going to save you?" she snaps. "Because you're not getting out on brains alone, and you know it."

He looks away, jaw set. "What's your point, Angelique?"

She softens, just a fraction. "We could help. For once, we could do something that matters. No one would have to know. We could fix it—fix all of it. Get rid of the food stamps, get Mom off our backs, maybe even give Jacob and Marcel a real shot."

He doesn't answer right away. Instead, he kicks a bottle cap across the ground, watches it skitter to the curb. The silence between them is thick, full of memories neither one wants to acknowledge: the times Beth wept behind a closed door, the night Wilbur broke his hand punching a wall because the mortgage people called again, the mornings when the fridge was so empty it echoed.

"I'm not stupid," Alphonse says at last. "You think they're just going to hand you the package and walk away? You think there aren't cops watching? Or other crews? You're not built for this, Angelique."

She grins, fierce and clean. "Neither are they. That's the point. They need someone invisible. Someone who doesn't look like trouble."

He studies her face, searching for cracks. He finds none.

"Fine," he says. "Say you do it. Then what? You hand off the drugs, get paid, and then what? You do it again? And again? Where does it stop?"

She shrugs, not pretending to know. "It stops when we have enough."

"And what's enough?"

She almost says a number, but the truth is, she doesn't know. There's never enough—not in this world.

The low growl of a forklift echoes from the factory down the block. A flock of pigeons erupts from the roof, startled into flight. The wind shifts, bringing with it the sharp sting of hot tar and old motor oil.

Alphonse sighs. "You already decided, didn't you?"

She nods. "I just need you to help me."

He stares at her for a long moment, then lets his arms fall to his sides. "If you're doing this, I'm not letting you go alone."

Relief and triumph flood her so quickly it leaves her unsteady. She touches his shoulder—a rare gesture—and says, "Thank you."

He shrugs it off, but not before she feels the tremor under his skin.

"Just promise me," he says, voice barely above a whisper, "if it goes bad, you run. Don't look back."

She nods, and the promise is both an oath and an admission.

They stand there in the shadow of the warehouse, the world suddenly small enough to fit in the space between them. Above, the sky is gridded with telephone wires, a pattern so rigid it almost looks deliberate.

Angelique looks up, and for the first time in weeks, she feels like she could break free.

The third time Angelique checks her watch, only four minutes have passed. The hands shiver on the dial, caught between the certainty of hours and the slippery trick of nerves. She and Alphonse loiter outside the Ben Franklin Dollar store, close enough to the shopping district that nobody looks twice, but far enough off the main drag that every car headlight, every passing voice, feels like a surveillance camera turned their way.

She's dressed the part—jeans with no rips, jacket borrowed from Beth's closet, hair brushed and pulled back so tight her scalp aches. Alphonse wears his oldest windbreaker, hood up, hands deep in the kangaroo pocket. They stand close, but not too close; the unspoken rule is that you never look like you're waiting for anything.

She's rehearsed the script a hundred times since last night. She's ready for the code word, the handoff, the way the world is supposed to lurch and then settle into a new order. But the longer they wait, the less real it feels. Angelique picks at a cuticle, draws blood, wipes it on the inside of her sleeve.

Alphonse whispers, "We should bounce."

She shakes her head, sharp and small. "Five more minutes."

He shrugs, but the tension is in his shoulders, the set of his jaw. He's scanning the cars, the shop windows, the silhouettes behind the glass.

The sun has already started to set, though the city glows on, burning its own daylight. A distant siren loops through the blocks, then fades. Two women exit the store, arms full of plastic bags, arguing about whose coupons are worth more. Behind them, the door swings shut, chimes jangling, and that's when she sees him—the broker.

He's younger than she expected, maybe nineteen, with a runner's build and the flat stare of someone who has seen a lot and cared about none of it. His jaw is square, his eyes unreadable. A thin scar runs through his right eyebrow, and his lips are cut into a permanent scowl. He approaches with the slow, measured pace of someone who never hurries, not for anything.

He glances at Alphonse first, as if confirming that the muscle is where it should be. Then his gaze lands on Angelique. "You Peach?"

She hesitates, then nods. "Yeah."

He produces a packet—a little ziplock, pressed tight as a button, sealed with a strip of blue tape. He holds it in his palm, but does not offer it.

"Where's the drop?"

Angelique swallows, then jerks her chin toward the newspaper box across the street. "Behind the Tribune stand."

He gives a single, satisfied nod. "You know the deal?"

She nods again, and this time her hands don't shake. "Show me the money."

He produces an envelope, holds it up like a dealer showing the last card. "After."

For a moment, nobody moves. The lights of the liquor store flicker to life, painting the sidewalk in false gold. The moment feels like it could last forever, but then Alphonse breaks the tension.

"You want to do this or not?" he mutters, just loud enough for the broker to hear.

The scarred boy's smile is thin, almost gentle. "You got it, little man." He glances up and down the street, then motions for Angelique to follow. She does.

They reach the newspaper box. Angelique slips the packet into the slot, slides her hand out, and waits.

The broker kneels, retrieves it, and inspects the seal. Satisfied, he counts out the bills—fifties and twenties, a hundred at a time— and tucks the envelope into her jacket pocket.

"That's it," he says, and he's already walking away, hands shoved deep into his coat.

The whole thing takes less than thirty seconds. Angelique is left standing on the curb, hand pressed to the envelope, head buzzing like she's just shotgunned a Red Bull. Alphonse stares after the broker, as if memorizing his walk, his gait, the swing of his arms.

They don't talk. Not at first. They walk, side by side, through the evening traffic and the rush of city people with places to be. The air is cold, electric. Angelique feels it all in her blood, a thrill that drowns out fear, regret, everything but the sense that she is finally, absolutely alive.

Three blocks later, they duck into an alley behind the donut shop, the neon sign above them bleeding pink onto the wet pavement. Angelique opens the envelope with shaking hands, peels back the edges, and fans the bills. The cash is crisp, new, smelling faintly of ink and ozone. She counts it once, then again: five hundred, right on the nose.

Alphonse lets out a slow whistle. "Damn."

She laughs, breathless. "Told you."

They stand in the alley, backs to the wall, just two kids counting money in the dark, and for a minute, nothing else matters.

Then Alphonse says, "We should split it. Fifty-fifty."

Angelique gives him a look. "What, you think I can't handle it?"

He shrugs. "I just don't want you getting greedy."

She wants to say something sharp, but she holds her tongue. Instead, she pulls out two bills and hands them to him. "Happy?"

He grins. "Yeah."

They stow the money in their socks, their shoes, wherever it will fit. Then, without another word, they melt back into the street, shoulders squared, chins up.

As they walk, Angelique looks over her shoulder. The church steeple is visible from here, just a white spike against the evening sky. She wonders if Wilbur is still there, polishing the pews, or maybe sitting in his office, praying for a miracle.

She smiles, a secret, wicked thing.

"This is just the beginning," she whispers.

They keep walking, and with every step, the church grows smaller, the city bigger. Soon, they are just two more shadows lost in the blur of streetlights, the old world dissolving behind them.

CHAPTER 12

The streetlights come alive in their appointed order, flickering to pale life as if reluctant to illuminate another evening. Emeryville at dusk is all muscle memory: the crumple of warehouses against the horizon, the stitched-together blocks of low-slung homes and chain-link, the flat, chemical taste of air settling after a day's labor. Jacob and Marcel walk home on the margin of a four-lane street, their shadows keeping pace across the vandalized glass and tar. There's almost no traffic, just the slow drip of people moving from job to job, or from job to nowhere, or from one shadow to the next.

The world is turning navy blue. Overhead, the last birds knife their way west. Marcel says nothing, which is unusual; he's usually a running mouth, a metronome of opinion and petty complaint. But tonight he moves in silence.

Jacob keeps his hands in his pockets, eyes flicking from sidewalk to street and back again. He's scanning for something—not danger, exactly, but significance, a sign the day won't be just another repeat of the last. He catches Marcel glancing at him, waiting for a joke, a nudge, any acknowledgment that they are more than just two bodies in motion. He gives none.

They round the corner by the old battery plant. The building is half-collapsed, windows gummed with dirt and decades-old stickers, its presence both a warning and a landmark. Across the street, a pair of silhouettes come into view, outlined by the sodium-yellow flood of a parking lot lamp.

Angelique walks with Alphonse at her side, both dressed like tomorrow will judge them by what they wore tonight. Angelique's hair is up, her step measured and sharp. Alphonse keeps his head down, but even from across the avenue, Jacob can see the way he clutches his jacket close, left wrist flexed just so, as if to broadcast the watch gleaming on his arm.

But it's the shoes that matter. Angelique's sneakers are blindingly white, out-of-the-box perfect, soles thick enough to level the whole city. Alphonse wears gold, bright enough to signal a rescue chopper.

Marcel is first to speak, voice cracking with disbelief. "Is that them?"

"Yeah," says Jacob, low. He doesn't slow down, doesn't look directly, but watches them out of the corner of his eye. He notes the newness, the shine, the deliberate way Angelique steps around puddles.

The siblings cross at the light, passing within arm's reach. Angelique's eyes flicker over them, then settle somewhere just behind Jacob's shoulder. She smiles, not unkindly, but with a practiced grace that says she is both of this world and above it. Alphonse flashes a crooked smile, then glances away, embarrassed by his own presence.

Jacob wants to say something—call them out, maybe, or ask where they got the money. But the words jam in his throat, clogging with the knowledge that any answer would only confirm what he already suspects. He settles for a tight nod.

Marcel, more reckless, says, "Damn, you won the lottery?"

Angelique barely breaks stride. "Good things come to those who hustle," she says, not even looking back.

Alphonse mumbles something, but it's lost in the hiss of the streetlight.

They keep moving, but the impression lingers: Angelique and Alphonse, glowing at the edge of the night, like saints or traitors. Jacob feels a heat rise behind his ears, a mixture of envy and something worse. He waits until they're out of sight before letting his jaw unclench.

Jacob shrugs. "It's whatever."

But it isn't. Not for Marcel. He quickens his pace, fists balled, mouth pinched tight. They walk a block in silence, then another, before the they reach the corner store—a squat, low-lit market with bars on the windows and an "ATM INSIDE" sign that flickers, unreliable. The parking lot is empty except for a line of ten-speeds, leaned and abandoned near the dumpster.

Marcel veers toward the bikes. "Let's check it out," he says, already halfway across the lot.

Jacob follows, reluctantly. The bikes are nothing special, a few missing chains, a mix of bald tires and faded paint. But near the door, clustered around the pay phone, is a trio of older boys. They are high-school age, maybe older, their faces half-hidden by hoodies and the late sun. Each wears a red bandana, either tied at the throat or hanging from a belt loop. Jacob knows the code; he's heard it whispered enough times in the halls, seen the evidence in scribbled graffiti and bathroom mirrors.

The one in the center is taller, his posture loose but charged, like a waiting dog. Darius. Jacob recognizes him from the basketball courts, from the fights behind the gym, from the way teachers say his name with a visible exhale. Darius is not handsome, but he has a smile that makes you want to follow him, or run.

Marcel, undeterred, walks right up to the line. He touches one of the bikes, fingers running along the handlebar, as if judging its weight.

"Don't," Jacob mutters, but Marcel ignores him.

Darius sees them. His smile is slow, deliberate. "Yo," he says. "You got business here?"

Marcel shrugs, gestures to the bikes. "Just looking. My brother wants one."

Darius glances at Jacob, appraising. "That so?"

Jacob meets his gaze, tries to flatten his voice. "We're good."

The two lieutenants flanking Darius don't move, but their eyes narrow. One taps a rhythm on his thigh, the other chews a toothpick.

Darius steps forward, blocking the sidewalk. "Ain't no harm in looking," he says, voice syrupy. "But you gotta pay up if you break something."

Marcel grins. "We ain't breaking shit."

Darius looks at Jacob again. "You his keeper?"

Jacob hesitates. "He does what he wants."

"That's right," says Marcel, and Jacob hears the pride, the hunger for approval.

Darius laughs, soft and short. "You got balls. I like that."

The second in command, the one with the toothpick, says, "They from the church family. The King kids."

Darius's eyes sharpen. "For real? Your old man's the preacher?"

Jacob nods, not sure if it's an accusation or a compliment.

Darius leans in, drops his voice. "You ever get tired of that shit?"

Jacob says nothing.

Darius waits, letting the quiet stretch between them. "Church boy life getting old? All that 'yes sir' and 'amen' bullshit?" Marcel's eyes flash with interest. "What else is there?"

Darius looks over at his crew, then back at the brothers. "You want to be somebody in this neighborhood, you gotta earn it. Can't be standing on the sidelines, waiting for handouts."

Marcel's foot taps the ground, hungry. "What do you do?"

Darius smiles again, and the toothpick guy joins in. "We look out for our own. Make money. Take care of business. Ain't no one pushing us around."

The first guy, who hasn't spoken yet, cracks his knuckles and stares at Jacob, waiting for a reaction.

Darius addresses Jacob directly now. "You want respect? You want people to know your name? You come see me. Tomorrow. After dark, behind the old factory."

Jacob knows the spot, knows the rumors of what happens there after the lights go out. He also knows what his father would say, what Beth would do if she caught them even talking to these boys. But something in Darius's tone, the confidence, the belonging, tugs at him. He feels the gravity of it, the black hole pull.

Marcel is already nodding. "We'll be there."

Darius gives a short salute. "Don't be late."

The three break apart, melting into the alley. The bikes are left leaning, untouched.

Marcel turns to Jacob, face flushed with adrenaline. "Damn. That was Darius."

Jacob mutters, "Yeah, I know."

"You think he's for real?"

Jacob doesn't answer. He starts walking, faster now, as if the distance between the store and home will dilute the memory.

Marcel jogs to catch up, still buzzing. "We going tomorrow?"

Jacob shrugs, then nods, almost imperceptible. "Yeah. We'll check it out."

Marcel whoops, then goes quiet, the anticipation settling between them like a shared secret.

They walk the rest of the way home, the city darkening by increments, every streetlight another witness. The sidewalks are empty, the air still, but in the distance, Jacob can hear the echo of laughter, the distant pop of a basketball, the pulse of a world he is not sure he wants to join.

He thinks of Angelique and Alphonse, their gold shoes and easy smiles, the way they moved through the city like nothing could touch them. He thinks of Darius, the promise of power, the danger of wanting more.

When they reach the block, the house is dark except for the kitchen light, Beth's silhouette visible behind the window. Jacob slows, lets Marcel go ahead, and for a moment, stands in the street, caught between the life he knows and the one that's been offered.

He wonders if there's a third option, or if the world is just a series of trades—one kind of pain for another, one kind of belonging for the next.

He does not have an answer. But as he climbs the porch steps, he feels the question settle into his bones.

In the morning, he will wake and pretend nothing has changed. But tonight, he lies awake, listening to the city's low hum, the weight of the invitation pressing down, sharp and cold as a bandana knot at the throat.

Fog sits heavy on the ground, swirling around Jacob's ankles as if the city intends to hold him here, just for the night. Behind the abandoned factory, the world is distilled to its elements: cold concrete, sharp metal, the low hum of machinery echoing from somewhere deep within the blocks. It is late—late enough that no one but the desperate, the faithless, or the sanctified would be out.

Darius is already waiting, his posture kingly on the half-crushed shipping crate, red bandana tied loose around his neck. Five others form a crescent behind him, their faces blurred by the mist and the haze of cheap cigarette smoke. Jacob recognizes some from the corner store, others only from legend: the ones teachers warn you about, the ones who have already learned how to put a world in motion with a single look.

Marcel stands beside Jacob, trembling, not with fear but with the kinetic charge of anticipation. He rubs his hands together, glancing at the other boys, measuring himself against their size and swagger. For a moment, he almost fits in.

Darius speaks, voice muffled but strong. "You made it. On time."

"We said we would," says Marcel, eager.

Jacob says nothing, keeping his hands jammed in the pockets of his jacket, fighting the urge to check the time.

Darius gestures at a box of spray paint, cans lined up like soldiers. "You want to be with us, you gotta make your mark. Here, tonight."

He motions to the cinderblock wall, already a palimpsest of tags —some new, some barely legible beneath layers of paint and grime.

Marcel steps forward, almost tripping in his haste. Darius tosses him a can—red, the color of warning. Marcel shakes it, the ball bearing inside clattering out a nervous staccato, then presses the nozzle to the wall.

He works quick, lines thick and sure, spelling out the letters with an artist's efficiency: RCP, three strokes tall and slanted like they're about to run away. He adds a flourish at the end, a whip of color that loops under the letters, then stands back, beaming.

Darius examines the work, then nods. "Not bad, little man. You got style."

The others grunt their approval, a chorus of short, satisfied sounds.

Darius points to Jacob. "Your turn."

Jacob hesitates, then takes a green can—he will not use red—and steps to the wall. His hands shake as he sketches out the symbol: a crown, basic and childish, but clear. He does not add a flourish.

Darius smirks. "You the prince now?"

Jacob shrugs, stepping back into the fog, hoping the wall will remember the tag better than the man who made it.

The ritual complete, Darius claps his hands, the sound sharp and final. "Now for the real work. You ready?"

Marcel nods, jaw set.

Jacob glances at his brother, then at the group. He is outnumbered, out-ritualed, but he nods anyway.

Darius leads them down a back alley, the crew moving as one body. At the edge of the lot, the lights of an electronics store buzz and sputter. The windows are barred, the door chained shut, but Darius pulls a crowbar from under his coat and hands it to the biggest boy—Hector, silent so far, whose arms are thick as pilings.

"You do the honors," says Darius, grinning.

Hector slides the bar between door and frame, wedges it, then leans his whole body weight until the lock snaps with a gunshot crack. The air inside is instantly colder, full of the metallic scent of new wires and ozone.

"Marcel, you're with Hector. Grab whatever you can carry. Jacob, you watch the street."

Marcel doesn't need to be told twice. He darts past the threshold, following Hector into the dark.

Jacob stands in the mouth of the alley, heart thumping. He can see the glow of the main avenue, can hear, somewhere, the laughter of people walking home from bars, the roll of distant trains. He checks the street, then checks again, eyes watering from the cold and the residual paint fumes.

Inside the store, glass shatters. A cascade of crash and curse. Jacob flinches, hands balling into fists. He thinks of Wilbur, of Beth, of the kitchen table and the rule about never bringing trouble home. He thinks of Angelique, her clean shoes, the promise of a different kind of power.

A figure bursts from the store—Hector, arms loaded with boxes. Marcel follows, clutching a smaller haul: a Bluetooth speaker, maybe, and a tangle of wires. His face is split by a crooked grin, triumph and disbelief.

Darius claps Marcel on the shoulder. "That's how you do it."

The boys form a huddle, passing around their prizes, voices low and urgent. Jacob stands apart, the lookout who never quite belonged, but Marcel waves him in.

"Check it out," says Marcel, holding up the speaker. "Brand new. Still got the tag."

Darius smiles, then pulls two red bandanas from his pocket. He ties one around Marcel's wrist, the knot tight and neat. The other, he offers to Jacob.

Jacob hesitates.

Darius says, "You earned it."

Jacob lets Darius tie the bandana, the fabric rough and still carrying the smell of machine oil. The knot is tight. It bites into his skin, a reminder that he is claimed now, marked.

The ritual concludes with a clasp—forearm to forearm, grip tight enough to bruise. The boys go around the circle, each repeating the gesture, a pledge made in skin and bone.

When it's Jacob's turn, he matches Darius's grip, holds it a second too long. Darius meets his eyes, searching, then nods.

"You're in," says Darius. "No going back."

Jacob nods, the truth of it stinging like the bandana. He looks at Marcel, who is practically vibrating with pride, the red knot shining in the dim light. For a second, Jacob feels the pull of belonging, the dark magnetism of the group.

But as they walk away from the factory, goods stashed under jackets, voices low and electric, Jacob's thoughts turn inward. He wonders how far the fog will follow them, how long before the city swallows them whole. He wonders if the crown he sprayed will last until morning, or if someone will paint over it, replacing it with another mark, another story.

Marcel skips ahead, already part of something bigger. Jacob hangs back, the red knot burning at his wrist.

He is in. There is no going back.

But he cannot shake the feeling that all of this—the tagging, the theft, the brotherhood—is just another kind of sermon, another script handed down from someone who once believed the world could be changed by force of will.

As the night closes in, Jacob listens to the rhythm of their steps, the scuff and echo, and tries to imagine what will become of the boys who follow Darius, what will become of those who don't.

He does not find an answer. Only the echo, and the memory of a crown, hastily drawn, dissolving in the rain.

Weeks peel away, each day wearing the same face as the last: school, the factory, the hollow drift of afternoons spent in parks and parking lots, boredom curdling into hunger. By now, Jacob and Marcel are regulars at the basketball courts, their status marked not just by the red bandanas but by the crowd that moves with them, a flotilla of new brothers and nearly-brothers, drawn to the centrifugal force of Darius's orbit.

Tonight, the courts buzz like a battery. Two rival crews circle the perimeter, faces half-lit by the busted halogens overhead, sneakers squeaking on asphalt, the chain-link fencing rattling with every rebound and curse. The air is thick with smoke, sweat, and the territorial reek of young men staking out their claim.

Jacob leans against the baseline, arms folded, watching the game but not watching. His focus is on the other side of the court, where the Richmond boys have gathered—blue bandanas, fresh tattoos, a language of their own, spoken in code and glances. There is a tension, always, but tonight it is a live wire.

Marcel stands beside Darius, chin up, laughing at a joke that rides the edge of threat. He's changed in the last weeks —shoulders broadened, voice dropped, every gesture sharper and more intentional. Jacob barely recognizes his brother, sometimes.

The ball slams off the backboard, bounces to center. A Richmond boy—tall, whip-thin, with a scar like an exclamation point on his cheek—snatches it, pivots, and drains a jumper from the elbow. He lets the shot hang, then stares down Darius's crew, smirk like a knife.

"You see that?" he calls. "Ain't nobody stopping us tonight."

Darius rolls his eyes, waves him off. "Talk is cheap, son."

The game resets. But the lines are drawn now; every possession is a referendum, every point a test of will. Trash talk escalates, bodies bang harder, fouls go uncalled and then, finally, unpunished.

It happens in a blur—one minute, a fast break; the next, a shoulder check that sends the ball spinning free and the blue bandana boy into the fence. He bounces off, comes up swinging. Darius's crew responds as one body, surging onto the court, Marcel in the lead.

Jacob watches, frozen, as the world tips.

The first punch lands with a hollow pop, knuckles to cheekbone. Blood leaps out in a perfect arc, staining the concrete. The blue bandana crew floods the court, fists and elbows and knees, every weapon available.

Marcel is in the thick, his eyes wide and bright, a wild grin splitting his face. He locks arms with the scarred boy, wrestling him down, then shoves his head into the fence with a force that surprises even him. The sound is sick, metal ringing against bone.

Jacob wants to yell, to pull his brother out, but his voice fails. Instead, he stands at the edge, hands clenching and unclenching, as the fight churns and shifts.

A brick appears—no one sees who throws it—but it whistles past Jacob's head, glancing off the post and shattering a fluorescent tube. The court goes half-dark, the world now just a theatre of shadows and silhouettes.

Then, the siren: at first just a rumor in the night, then close, urgent, rising above the shouts.

"Cops!" someone yells. The crews break apart, scattering like birds.

Jacob sprints, breath raw in his throat. He finds Marcel halfway across the parking lot, blood streaking his temple, hands shaking but alive.

They run together, legs pumping, lungs burning. Behind them, the siren grows, then recedes, swallowed by the maze of streets.

Wilbur kneels in the nave of Triumph Church, body dwarfed by the empty pews. The lights are out, save for a single bulb above the altar, casting a pool of jaundiced gold. His hands are laced, knuckles white, head bowed so low his forehead nearly grazes the old wood rail.

He prays not with words, but with the muscle memory of decades—every tendon and joint straining for a sign, an answer, some small reversal of fate. The silence is a living thing, crowding out the old hymns and even the memory of them.

At last he speaks, voice hoarse: "Lord, I can't reach them. I can't hold them. If you are listening, send me something. Anything. I'm begging."

The plea rings out, unanswered, and settles into the dust.

Wilbur stays there, motionless, until his legs go numb.

Beth sits at the kitchen table, her ledger open, pen hovering above the page. The columns are blank tonight, the rows empty; she cannot bring herself to record the week's accounts. Across from her, a prayer journal—gifted by a woman at church, inscribed "for your daily walk"—lies unopened, the spine still creaking from the bookstore.

She tries to write. She tries to pray. But nothing comes.

Instead, she listens for the sounds that have always defined her world: the shuffle of feet on the porch, the click of the door, the hush of voices in the next room. She listens and waits, because that is what mothers do, when they have nothing else.

In the bedroom, Jacob sits on the edge of his cot, the red bandana loose on his wrist, a dark bloom already soaking the fabric where a rival's fist clipped bone. Marcel sits beside him, stripped to the waist, chest marked by fresh bruises and a line of drying blood along his eyebrow.

Marcel grins, recounting the fight in urgent whispers. "Did you see that? Dude tried to choke me out, but I flipped him—just like that. He's not gonna mess with us again."

Jacob doesn't answer. He flexes his hand, watching the skin around his knuckles swell and purple. It hurts, more than he will admit.

Marcel keeps talking, each sentence brighter than the last, his pride filling the room.

But for Jacob, the night is a weight. He can't stop seeing the look on Marcel's face—the wildness, the pleasure—and he wonders if this is what becoming a man means. He wonders if there is any way back.

He lies down, pulling the blanket to his chin. The sheets smell faintly of paint, sweat, and loss.

He closes his eyes, but sleep will not come. Outside the window, another siren sings the city's lullaby.

He wonders if anyone is listening.

In the other room, Beth stares at the blank page, willing it to reveal the next move. The pen hovers, then falls.

The ledger stays empty. But in the silence, a prayer finally forms —not a request, not a demand, just a single word, repeated over and over, until it no longer sounds like language at all, but like the heartbeat of a woman who refuses to be broken.

Please. Please. Please.

On the kitchen wall, the clock ticks forward, unbothered.

In the church, Wilbur's prayers dissolve into let the dark.

And in the bedroom, two brothers lie side by side, neither certain if they are more themselves or less.

Outside, the world spins on, indifferent.

The night is a wound that will not close.

In the weeks that followed, Jacob's sense of time slipped loose from the old tethers—Sunday sermons and school bells and Beth's relentless tallying of days. The church lost its dominion over him, if it ever really held any. He still went, of course, the way a body went through digestion: slow, unstoppable, full of processes no one asked to understand. But the real tempo of his life now thrummed to the pulse of the crew. School days were a blur of hours, a series of obsidian notes on the ledger that mattered least, and evenings belonged to Darius.

He learned things. He learned how to cut through the chain fence behind the old recycling plant, where the city dumped broken office chairs and the husks of TVs. He learned the difference between a warning look and the kind that meant a fight would start in the next three seconds. He learned not to run if you were getting chased—unless you knew, absolutely, you would not get caught. He learned how to smoke a blunt without coughing it up. He learned you did not ever, under any circumstances, let Hector get a grip on your neck.

Most of all, Jacob learned to make his face blank when they sprayed paint on a rival tag, or when Marcel got sent first into a bodega to size up the clerk, or when the haul was thin and Darius's temper snapped cold and precise as a scalpel. He learned that standing still in the middle of trouble could feel more powerful than moving away from it.

The red bandana left a weal on his wrist, but he rarely let it show.

Sometimes, after a night out, Jacob would just walk, city blocks ticking past beneath numb feet, the spark of adrenaline simmering to a low, manageable ache. The houses here were different from the South, geometry sharper, the yards divided from the sidewalk by fences barely tall enough to keep out a rabbit. Every few weeks he tried to recall the smell of Arkansas grass, or the hush that fell right before a storm at dusk, but it was like remembering the taste of a different body's mouth.

He came home late on a school night, the winter sun already wrung dry and the sodium lights starting their slow, malignant crawl over the block. Beth was still up, her back to the door, cutting coupons from the circulars at the kitchen table. The look on her face when he crossed the threshold—he had not seen that look since he broke a neighbor's window with a baseball at age six, since Wilbur made him apologize and shake the man's hand. It was not really anger. It was a calculation, a long division problem with a remainder she refused to carry.

"Where's Marcel?" she asked, not even turning. Her hands were still, scissors poised in the air.

He shrugged. "Still at the gym. Said he'd walk home."

"No he didn't." The scissors snapped through a coupon for twenty-five cents off ground beef. "You're lying."

He didn't answer. The lie, he realized, was not about Marcel but about the very concept of coming home.

She finished the stack, then set the scissors down, deliberate. "I need you to be in this house when it's dark," she said, voice somber and knowing. She waited, and when he didn't flinch, she said, "You still want to live here, or you want to go off and be a big man for someone else?"

He stared at the wall clock. The sweep-hand thudded past minute after minute while she watched him. He said, "I'll be in by midnight." He meant to leave it at that, but when she said, "You sure about that?" his mouth moved faster than his brain: "Why do you even care if I come home?"

She made a face. "You don't know? Try me." She stacked the clippings, leaned back, and let the silence do the work.

He didn't know how to answer, so he just stood there until the silence filled the room. When she went back to her coupons, the only sound was the crisp snick of blades slicing newsprint, each coupon a tiny mercy withheld.

In his room, he found his bed stripped and a pile of newly thrifted bedsheets dumped at the footboard. The pattern—cheerful sunflowers—was clearly for a child. He thought about pulling off the sheets, but at the last second decided to just lie down, sideways on top, keeping his shoes on and his jacket zipped. It was cold in here—no heat ticked through the vents after ten p.m.—but the jacket would do. He lay still and listened to the world narrowing around him, street noise and the faint hum of the fridge and the twin heartbeats of his parents arguing softly in their bedroom.

He could tell what kind of argument it was by the cadence of their voices. Tonight's was the low, sustained kind; no yelling, just the soft murmur of things that could wait until morning because neither side wanted to give up the upper hand. He closed his eyes and tried to imagine what they might be saying about him, then gave up, distracted by the charge still in his arms from the court fight, the ringing throb of where his hand had smashed into a rival's jaw.

He pressed his knuckles to his mouth. They tasted like copper and spray paint.

Marcel didn't come home until almost two. He woke Jacob with the sharp, mechanical chirp of the window lock. Marcel climbed through, careful to close the glass with both hands, then shed his backpack and shoes in one practiced motion before rolling onto the cot. They lay head-to-toe, as they used to when they were little, in a way that made sharing one blanket seem like a treaty.

"Tomorrow we're going for the snack shop," whispered Marcel, low and close, as if the darkness might swallow his excitement. "Hector says he can get the register open if I hold the door. Said there's a box and everything."

"Okay," whispered Jacob, not because he was scared, but because he knew how much it mattered to Marcel to have someone say it back.

Marcel grinned into the darkness, kicking his feet at the end of the cot as though pent-up energy would burn holes through the soles of his socks. The night was a secret pact between them, the kind boys forged in the intervals between fear and bravado, and Jacob could not help but feel the weight of it pressing on the narrow slice of mattress that separated their bodies. He lay awake, counting the seconds between Marcel's excited breaths, listening to the city unspool its catalog of midnight, and wondering how long it would take before the next escalation, the next dare, the next test of what the world could be made to give.

CHAPTER 13

Angelique sat at the kitchen table, staring at the faded daffodil wallpaper as her fingers traced the chipped mug's cold rim. Slanting afternoon light sliced through the window in stripes, illuminating swirling dust; the house was unnervingly quiet except for the ticking clock and Beth's footsteps down the hall. Her thoughts drifted back to Hector.

It had started innocently enough—Hector helping her carry groceries, shy smiles exchanged across the linoleum floor. Late that summer, their whispers had grown bolder: secret dinners at his tiny apartment, laughter in the dark, skin pressed against skin until the world beyond those four walls ceased to exist. Angelique had never known desire like it. She remembered how safe she'd felt in his arms, his breath warm against her neck. He'd held her close when she confessed, trembling, that she was afraid of what came next.

When the test turned positive, panic had flared in her chest. She'd spent nights crying into the pillow, hands trembling as she called the clinic. The nurse had been brusque; the antiseptic sting of bleach lingered in every corridor, mingled with the faint scent of wilting carnations. She'd lain on the narrow table, heart hammering, as a doctor's calm voice told her what she already knew she must do.

She hadn't told Hector. He would have begged her to keep the child; she'd adored him for that fierce tenderness. But she couldn't—couldn't burden him, couldn't bring another mouth to feed in a world that already felt too heavy. So she'd walked out alone, coat wrapped tight, each step home heavier than the last.

Now, as Beth's shadow darkened the doorway, Angelique forced her breath to slow. Her stomach churned hollowly; her body trembled beneath the thin cotton of her blouse.

"Angelique! In here, now." Beth's voice cut through the silence, sharp and unrelenting.

She stood and entered the living room, heart slamming against her ribs. Beth stood rigid, arms crossed, jaw clenched. Wilbur hovered beside her, Marcel leaned against the wall with wide, horrified eyes, Jacob lingered in the doorway, and even Alphonse —who hadn't spoken to her in weeks—looked up, worry etched on his face.

Clutched in Beth's hand was a crumpled appointment card from the clinic on San Pablo. "Explain this," she demanded, voice throbbing with rage.

Angelique's throat went dry. "It's nothing—just a doctor's visit."

"Don't play dumb," Beth shot back. "They called for a follow-up. Your father got the message. You went to that clinic."

Wilbur's voice wavered. "Is it true? You went alone?"

Angelique nodded, unable to meet his gaze.

Beth's face went white. "After everything we've done for you— after all we taught you—how could you think we wouldn't find out?" She stepped forward, chest heaving. "You kept this from us? You killed your own child?"

Angelique's composure shattered. "I didn't kill anyone—I did what I had to do. I'm sorry."

Beth's hand lashed out, striking Angelique across the cheek. The room froze. Angelique staggered but didn't fall; her hand flew to her reddening skin.

"Sorry?" Beth spat, then struck again—harder this time —beating at Angelique's arms and shoulders with frantic desperation, each blow fueled by betrayal and grief. Wilbur lunged to intervene, but Beth shoved him away. Marcel covered his face; Jacob and Alphonse rushed forward, helpless.

When at last Beth's fury spent itself, she sank to her knees. Angelique crumpled to the floor, tears mingling with the sting of bruising skin. The house fell silent, broken by choking sobs and the ragged sound of Beth's own crying.

Angelique lay curled at her feet, the secret she'd carried now an open wound shared by them all.

Wilbur lowered himself beside Beth, his knees popping, the old injury from the loading dock howling as his weight hit the floor. He reached for her, but Beth jerked away, fists clamped to her skirt, face pressed flat to her knees. For a moment, Angelique thought her mother would never look up again, that she'd folded herself so small she might finally vanish. But then Beth's voice rose from the dark space between elbows and chest—a sound more animal than human, low and raw and pulsing with everything she'd refused to name.

Wilbur tried again, hand trembling as it hovered at the small of her back. "Let's all sit. Let's be… let's just breathe."

Nobody moved. The pain was still echoing in everyone's bones, the shape of Beth's anger stamped into the silence. Marcel stayed glued to the wall, one hand covering his mouth, the other white-knuckled behind his back. Jacob's eyes skipped from Wilbur to the rug to his sister's face and away again, as if contact might scorch him. Alphonse crept closer, cautious, and dropped into a crouch at Angelique's side, but when she turned her head to meet him, he flinched like he'd been hit too.

Beth's crying slowed, but her words spat out in uneven bursts. "This... this is what the world wanted. To take my children. Turn us into animals. Liars. Murderers. I raised you better than this, Angelique. I did."

Angelique wiped her mouth, the taste of iron and shame sticky on her tongue. The skin where Beth's hand landed burned, but deeper than that, the ache hollowed out her chest. She pulled her knees up, pressing them so hard to her ribs it hurt to breathe.

Wilbur's prayers trickled out, barely louder than the sound of shoes scuffing carpet. "Lord, show us mercy, hold us together, don't let us break..." His hand trembled against Beth's shoulder, but she shook him off, focusing her gaze on Angelique with a grief so pure it was almost holy.

"Did you even think?" Beth demanded, her voice cracked and gone thin. "Not about us—not even about him—but about that soul you threw away? Did you think what it means?"

Angelique wanted to lie, to say yes, to say she'd done the math and weighed all the suffering and found it balanced. But she could only shake her head. There was no number for this, no calculus for loss. "I didn't know what else to do, Mama," she said, voice catching. "I couldn't... I couldn't have a baby now. Not with Hector's life, not with school, not with how things are." Each word made the room smaller. "I'm sorry. I wish it—I wish it didn't have to be like this."

Beth crumpled further, shoulders shaking. "I loved you," she whispered. "I loved all of you. I tried to make you different. I tried so hard."

Wilbur's voice was flat, resignation already at the edges. "She's still our blood," he said, but the words skittered across the floor.

"I'm sorry," Angelique repeated, voice small and tight. "You don't know what it's like. I just... couldn't."

Beth squeezed her eyes shut. "That was part of us, girl. That child was hope. And you chose..." She trailed off, the words refusing to rise.

"I chose not to drown." Angelique's tone surprised even herself: not sharp, not angry, but flat, like the surface of a lake on a windless day. "I did what I thought I had to."

Alphonse bent to scoop up the appointment card, folding it into a neat square, as if by putting the evidence away he could undo the moment.

A month oozed by.

On the other side of town, Alphonse leaned on a splintered bus bench outside the closed pharmacy, arms wrapped around his knees, watching the sodium bulb above the lot sputter in and out. He had not been inside the King house for three days. Not since the shouting, not since the news about Angelique's not-so-secret abortion passed through the family like a stinging wind. He found himself, on nights like this, migrating to the places where the light was thin and the only company was the echo of his own decisions. He would walk the perimeter of the shopping center, past the shuttered nail salons and the windows taped with posters for deals that had long expired, until his feet ached or until he ran into someone worth talking to.

It was on one of these circuits that he first saw her—leaning, almost boneless, against the chain-link fence behind the liquor store, hands nested in the pockets of a dirty pink windbreaker, eyes wild and searching. She moved the way moths moved, nervous and voracious, never letting herself be still long enough to get caught in anything but the blur of her own need. She was humming to herself, some half-tuned melody from a cartoon, and when she saw him she didn't flinch or look away—she just stared, lips parted, as if waiting for him to speak first.

He did not remember how the conversation started. He only remembered the oddness of her presence, the way her voice would jerk from too-loud to a barely-there mumble, the way she never said her real name but answered to Trudy, or any of the names the neighborhood had pressed upon her. She was not like the other girls he'd known. There was nothing ornamental about her; she was all nerve endings and improvisation, a bundle of accidents in a world that dealt almost exclusively in intentions.

The first night, Alphonse watched her from a distance, trying to piece together the choreography of her habits. He saw her pluck cigarette butts from the gutter, pinch the filters between ink-stained fingers, and smoke them all the way down. He saw her barter a can of Sprite for a half-eaten donut with a homeless man who slept in the alley behind the pharmacy. He saw her vanish for a half hour and return with her windbreaker zipped to the chin, eyes glassy and rimmed with pink. She never stayed in one place for long, but she always returned to the fence, as if it were a starting block for some future race only she could see.

The second night, he brought a pack of Newports and waited. She arrived just past midnight, shuffling in mismatched shoes, her hair even more tangled than he remembered. He offered her a cigarette and she took it, sniffing it suspiciously before lighting up, her hands shaking so badly that he had to cup his own around hers to get the spark to catch. She exhaled, then smiled at him—a thin, grateful thing that looked as though it might snap at any second.

"She's a mess," he told himself, but the words sounded hollow, like something he'd been made to memorize for a test he never signed up for. Her mess was somehow magnetic. It made his own feel less solitary.

Tonight, she was already at the fence when he arrived. She was humming again, the same half-melody, and her eyes were darting, scanning, never resting for more than a second. He stood a few paces away, trying to catch her attention, but she was somewhere else entirely, so he waited, rocking on his heels and watching the pattern of her movements.

Alphonse was seventeen then, restless and sharp-edged, drawn to broken things with the stubborn hope that he might fix them. He handed her a cigarette one night, and she took it with trembling fingers, giving him a smile that flickered on and off like a faulty porch light.

They started meeting in secret—behind the shuttered laundromat, under the humming streetlamps, in the alleys where the city's noise faded to a dull, hollow ache. Trudy's moods shifted like the weather: some days she was giddy and wild, pulling Alphonse through the streets in the vain hope of adventure; other days she shrank from his touch, her voice small and scared, mumbling about shadows and voices only she could hear.

Still, Alphonse kept coming back. He brought her food and spare change, tried to make her laugh, tried to keep the worst of the world at bay. Sometimes, in the thin, gray hour before dawn, she would curl against him and cry silently, her body shaking with old griefs she couldn't name.

On a chilly autumn evening as they huddled together under the dim streetlights, Alphonse leaned in closer to share warmth. Their eyes met and they shared a nervous smile. Timidly at first, their lips found each other's in a slow motion. As if time had stopped for them both in this moment of connection. Trudy's soft hands clenched his shirt while Alphonse gently held her waist as they shared in passion.

As they parted from their kiss, their foreheads rested against one another as their breaths mingled together. They found comfort and safety within each other's embrace. The intimacy between them continued to grow with each meeting beneath those streetlights – a secret escape from the harsh reality they were both trapped in.

When she first told him she was pregnant, Alphonse felt both dread and pride—a rush of responsibility that left his hands shaking. He promised her he'd take care of things, tried his best to keep her safe, but by the final months she barely let him near, disappearing for days at a time, returning thinner, more haunted.

She gave birth in a rundown county hospital, alone except for a tired nurse and the old blanket Alphonse had left with her weeks before. Alphonse arrived just in time to see the baby—a dark-skinned girl with a cap of soft black hair and eyes that followed every shadow. Trudy wouldn't hold her, wouldn't even look at her.

"She yours now," Trudy said, voice flat, gaze fixed on the cracked ceiling tile. "Don't give her my name. She ain't got nothing from me but trouble."

Alphonse gathered the baby in his arms, feeling the fierce, raw love that surprised him with its strength. He named her Manon, a name he'd once seen in a storybook, whispered to her as she blinked up at him, tiny fist wrapping tight around his finger.

He brought Manon home, hoping for a fresh start, not knowing the burden he'd asked her to carry. But in that first moment, holding her close, Alphonse let himself believe, if only for a breath, that broken things could be made new.

Beth found Alphonse waiting on the porch, the sky still gray with dawn. He sat hunched, elbows on knees, rocking gently—a tiny bundle swaddled in a borrowed hospital blanket cradled in his arms. Manon slept against his chest, her breaths shallow and quick, a tuft of black hair peeking from the blanket's edge.

Beth stood in the doorway, arms folded, her gaze cutting through the morning hush. "What you doing here so early, Alphonse? And whose baby is that?" Her voice was sharp, but softer than usual.

He didn't look up. "Trudy gone," he said, voice hoarse from a sleepless night. "Won't even look at the baby. She's been gone three days."

Beth stepped closer, taking in the sight of her son—so often reckless, now small and trembling, clutching this child like she was the last good thing in the world. Beth's heart twisted, but she kept her face stern.

"You got a plan, boy?" she asked.

Alphonse shook his head. "She needs more than I got. She need somebody steady. Somebody who knows how to raise a child."

Beth let the silence hang between them, her eyes settling on Manon's tiny face. The baby stirred, mouth rooting for comfort, and Alphonse instinctively rocked her, though his hands shook.

Beth sighed, low and heavy. "Bring her inside," she said at last, voice brooking no argument. "She need a bath. And a proper name."

Alphonse looked up, hope flickering in his eyes. "I named her Manon," he said quietly. "That's all I could give her."

Beth's lips pressed into a line, but she didn't argue. She led the way into the kitchen, clearing a space on the counter, gathering old flannel and warm water. Alphonse hovered in the doorway, watching as Beth washed Manon with practiced hands, her movements rough but careful.

When she finished, Beth bundled the baby in a clean towel, holding her for a long moment. "She's family," Beth said at last, eyes never leaving the tiny face. "Whatever your mistakes, she's blood. I'll see to her now. But you best get yourself together, Alphonse. You don't want her growing up thinking her daddy just ran off."

Alphonse nodded, shame and relief mingling in his face. He bent and pressed a kiss to Manon's cheek, whispering a promise he wasn't sure he could keep.

Beth watched him go, then turned her full attention to Manon. "You're mine now," she murmured, voice both a vow and a warning, as she carried the baby deeper into the house and into a future neither of them could yet see.

CHAPTER 14

Violence has a way of creeping slowly, then all at once—spreading out across days, leaving fractures that ripple through every corner of the city and the family that calls it home.

Jacob hadn't slept in weeks, and on that Friday evening the failing light turned San Pablo's curbs to ash and bone. Every building loomed like a sin he couldn't wash away. He felt hollow part of him craving resolution, part terrified of what that resolution might demand.

His trouble had started with simply enough: money owed by a greasy-haired operator who treated every deal like a game. Weeks of warnings and bravado-laced threats had earned only silence. Tonight, they'd agreed to meet on the front steps of his family home—a neutral ground, he'd thought, a place that might shame the man into paying. But Jacob's gut knotted the way it always did before everything went off the rails.

The man arrived with two skinny cronies in tow. The porch light cast their shadows large and jagged against the peeling clapboard. A loose gathering of neighbors edged close—old men with nothing left to lose, teenage girls trading dares, even a patrol car idling in voyeuristic curiosity. Jacob pressed his hands into his pockets, telling himself to stay calm. But the operator sneered, mocking Jacob's persistence, goading him with a slur aimed at Jacob's mother. The insult was a blade that severed restraint.

Fists flew. A bottle shattered against the railing. Pain bloomed in Jacob's forearm, then bit into his thigh when a jagged shard of glass cut deep. He tasted copper in his mouth as his fingers curled around the cold steel of the Beretta at his hip—the same gun he'd sworn he'd never touch except for emergencies. His mind screamed to stop, but adrenaline roared louder. He leveled the barrel and squeezed the trigger.

The shot cracked through the night like a warhead, rattling windows and drowning out the world. The operator staggered back, knees folding into the wooden step, before he pitched forward in a spray of red across the warped planks. Then came the eerie hush, broken only by the drip of blood onto concrete.

Jacob barely had time to stare before the patrol car's lights flooded the porch in harsh blues and reds. Officers poured out, weapons drawn, orders cutting the air like bayonets. Panic clutched his chest as a volley of rounds erupted—six bullets tore into him on the steps of the only home he'd ever known. One smashed through his chest, another opened his gut, a third shattered bone in his arm, a grazing shot riddled his shoulder, and a final slug carved fire down his back. He sagged against the railing, every breath an inferno.

"Get down! Hands where we can see them!" an officer barked as Jacob's vision spun kaleidoscopic. He collapsed to his knees in a spreading pool of his own blood, his world slanting off its axis. Weakness forced his arms upward; cuffed hands pressed cool steel into bruised flesh. Paramedics arrived at the top of the steps, voices urgent as they applied pressure to his wounds, but the pain was a blinding thunder.

"Jacob King, you're under arrest for homicide," an officer intoned, though Jacob could barely hear over the roar in his ears. Sirens wailed behind him, echoing against the silent houses on the block. Dawn's first light seeped through the siren glow—pale, tremulous, indifferent—mirroring the uncertain verdict that awaited him. Cuffed and bleeding on the threshold of everything that had once been safety, Jacob closed his eyes and wondered if any punishment could ever tip the balance of the scales in his fractured mind.

Monday night was choked with the fog and smog that blanketed Emeryville like a shroud. Marcel hated waiting. He lived in bursts: a sprint down the court, a flurry of dominoes, jokes that landed one beat too loud. Tonight, he'd stayed late at a friend's apartment off 66th, his fingers still sticky with barbecue sauce and the aftertaste of cheap beer souring his mouth. The buses always ran late on Mondays, and Marcel, bored by the pause, kicked at the curb, flicking pebbles and bottle caps at an imaginary hoop.

He felt eyes on him—he'd sensed their shadow all summer: looks at parties, signals from girls, threats scrawled on bus-stop glass. Now, even in the fog, Marcel recognized their car when it rolled up alongside the curb. Headlights off, doors opening to four shapes that lunged out. He told himself he'd waited for this showdown, but when a voice spat his name with raw venom, his knees wobbled. Words flew—insults, accusations—before a blade glinted, carving a line of light through the fog.

Adrenaline surged. Marcel caught the attacker's wrist, but the lunge drove the blade into the soft web of his left hand. Blood gushed, warm and sticky, slicking his shirt and fingers. Panic sharpened every sense. He remembered his father's advice about breaking grips—move with the force, not against it. Marcel twisted, wrenching the knife free and reversing its arc. Time slowed as the blade sank into his rival's chest with a hollow thunk. The boy's eyes went wide in disbelief, then he collapsed, limbs folding like a discarded puppet.

Silence fell. The others scattered into the mist. Marcel stood above the body, blood pooling around him. His heart thundered so loud he could barely hear the distant hum of cars. His legs gave out. He crumpled to the sidewalk, shivering, arms wrapped tight around his knees. He didn't try to run. When the police arrived, Marcel could only croak out the truth. He felt tears burning on his cheeks, humiliation nearly worse than the pain in his hand.

Alphonse felt the weight of this moment before he even arrived —Thursday before dawn, when the city's hush pressed against his ears like a whispering predator. He'd lied to Beth and Wilbur; said he was at a friend's house studying for a test. Instead, he'd followed the older boys from the Red Chilie Peppers to a back alley, roped into a quick handoff: a tiny bag, some crumpled bills, a deal he convinced himself would pass unnoticed.

Behind the shuttered taqueria, he tasted oil and onions dead in the air. Every step made his insides clench. The buyer—a skinny kid with rough stubble and eyes that looked decades older—hovered by the grease-smudged wall, glancing over Alphonse's shoulder. Alphonse's heart pounded so loudly he could almost hear his own ribcage crack. The buyer's hand drifted into his coat. Alphonse couldn't tell if he was pulling out cash or a gun. Panic tipped something inside him.

His fingers closed around the cold metal of the pistol Jacob had left him. His brain screamed for him to drop it, but reflex took over. He raised the weapon. The first shot screamed past the buyer's shoulder, shattering glass above the alley mouth. Fear fogged Alphonse's vision. He squeezed again. The second bullet found the buyer's neck. Alphonse stood frozen as the body slumped into a slick puddle.

Silence fell heavier than before. Alphonse's breathing rattled in his chest. He dropped the gun; it skidded across the pavement and rolled to rest against a discarded churro wrapper. He backed away until the alley's darkness gave way to streetlight. Mother's warning echoed in his mind: Stay away from trouble. His knees buckled and he vomited into a cracked planter.

He wandered, soaked in early-morning chill and guilt, invisible among waking commuters. Dawn bled pale yellow over rooftops, but nothing could wash away what he'd done in the night.

Each day, the news of the tragedies moved outward through Emeryville's concentric circles—first among the gangs and their satellites, then through the schools and churches, then finally, inevitably, into the homes of the city's gossips and watchful elders. The King name, once a source of grudging respect— a legacy built on decades of hard labor and quiet discipline— became a scourge.

By week's end, Emeryville was quieter than usual. On the streets, children played closer to home; in the church, voices dropped to thoughtful murmurs. Beth clutched her Bible, old grief mixing with new shame, while Wilbur sat silent at the kitchen table, staring at his hands, wondering where the foundation of his family had cracked—and if he'd ever be able to repair it.

It's morning in Emeryville, courthouse steps already swelling with a second congregation, not unlike the Sunday throngs Wilbur used to command, though here the attire is more funereal—dull suits, wrinkled slacks, the occasional shivering woman in bright polyester who looks as if she might flee at the first sound of the bailiff's voice. The King family advances up the stairs as if through a slow-moving storm, the boys flanking Wilbur, Beth and the girls trailing in their wake, all faces scrubbed and unsmiling. There is a brief, crackling moment when they hesitate at the threshold—Wilbur's hand hovers over the door, as if waiting for divine permission—and then they cross over, the world inside instantly colder, infused with the tang of bleach and institutional coffee.

The courthouse foyer is echo and marble. The elevator is out, so the family climbs the spiral staircase to the third floor, the rails sticky to the touch, every step sending a tremor through Beth's knees. She carries the Bible like a shield, thumb pressed hard into the gold-leafed margin, as if the right verse, if applied with enough force, might hold back what comes next.

Before Alphonse's trial, the fate of his older brothers had already been sealed. Jacob, convicted of manslaughter, received a fifteen-year sentence in San Quentin. Marcel, whose self-defense plea found little sympathy in the court, was handed ten years at Folsom. Their convictions cast a long shadow over the family, the news arriving in heavy, separate envelopes that Beth opened with trembling hands. By the time Alphonse faced the judge, the Kings were already accustomed to watching sons led away in chains, each sentence erasing another line of the future they once imagined.

Outside the courtroom, a crowd has already gathered, clustering in predatory knots around the double doors. A woman with a baby on her hip, whispering into a cell phone; two men in matching blue blazers, eyes darting over every new arrival; a boy with a skateboard and a busted lip, who looks up at the Kings with the expression of someone who has bet on the wrong side before. There is a smell of sweat and damp wool, the low buzz of anticipation as the hour approaches.

Angelique is late. She enters alone, jacket slung over her arm, hair pulled so tight it lifts her cheekbones, eyes forward. She does not look at the family, nor at the clusters of strangers who track her passage through the hallway. Instead, she plants herself against the wall, back straight, hands folded in her lap so the trembling will not be seen.

Wilbur moves to approach her, but Beth stops him with a glance. "She'll come when she's ready," she whispers, so quietly it barely vibrates the air. Wilbur nods, but the effort costs him; his shoulders wilt, and for a moment he seems to shrink inside his suit.

The bailiff calls for order. The doors yawn open, and the room pours in—a mass of bodies arranged in neat, adversarial rows, each seat a front row to the theater of consequences. The family sits together, except Angelique, who chooses the far end of the pew, as if proximity itself might be construed as complicity. Beth grips the Bible. Wilbur wipes his brow with a handkerchief, the gesture both nervous and futile.

When Alphonse is led into the room, there is a brief shudder of attention—a lifting of heads, the ripple of intake breath. He wears the orange jumpsuit with a certain irony, as if daring the assembly to see him as anything but a boy in borrowed clothes. His hair is cropped close, his face scrubbed and impassive. Only his eyes move, scanning the gallery, pausing on the family, then flicking away. He sits in the defendant's box with his back straight, fingers laced on the table, wrists unencumbered by cuffs; for this, the court has afforded him a rare dignity, though it seems more a courtesy to the spectators than the accused.

The judge enters—an old man, shrunken in his robes, but with eyes that catch every lie before it can cross the lips. The room stands, then settles, the hush so total that the click of the gavel is almost obscene.

The trial begins.

The prosecution is led by a woman with gray hair and a

voice like piano wire. She wastes no time on preliminaries, launching instead into a recitation of facts: the murder at the corner of Sixty-Sixth and San Pablo, the victim a known dealer, the transaction gone wrong. Surveillance footage: grainy, time-stamped, looping for the jury on a screen propped by an AV cart scavenged from a middle school. There is a still frame of Alphonse standing beneath a failing streetlamp, face obscured but posture unmistakable—one shoulder higher, one foot canted in, the same stance he used to assume at the breakfast table when he believed he had outsmarted the world.

The prosecutor leans into the evidence. Witnesses are called— a neighbor who heard the gun, a shopkeeper who saw "a black boy running like the devil himself was after him." Ballistics: the bullet matched to a cheap revolver, found three blocks away in a dumpster behind a taqueria. The weapon is displayed in a plastic bag, held aloft for the jury by a gloved hand, as if even the inanimate requires protection from contamination.

Alphonse never looks at the gun. He watches the witness box, eyes fixed and unblinking, as if memorizing the script for later review. His court-appointed lawyer—a man in a suit that predates Angelique's existence—raises objections at regular intervals, but the judge dismisses them with a weary flick of his fingers. The narrative builds, hour by hour, each detail layering atop the last until the room is thick with inevitability.

Beth sits motionless, lips pressed to the back of her hand, the Bible open to Psalms. Every now and then she marks a passage, as if the words might swell with enough meaning to crowd out the sound of the prosecutor's voice. Wilbur leans forward, elbows on knees, hands clasped so tight the knuckles lose all color. He mutters, sometimes, not in prayer but in inventory: checking each piece of evidence, counting the seconds it takes for the jury to react, auditing the slow erosion of hope.

Angelique keeps her face impassive. She does not flinch at the crime scene photos, nor at the description of the victim's final moments. Her fingers drum the side of the pew. She will not look at Beth, nor at Alphonse, nor at the jury. Her gaze is for the floor, or for the far wall where the clock ticks with a dull, incessant certainty.

When the prosecution rests, there is a perceptible slackening, as if the entire room has exhaled. The defense offers little in rebuttal—an alibi of convenience, the suggestion that the surveillance video could be anyone, the insinuation that the witness was too far away to distinguish a face. None of it lands; the judge's expression is unmoved; the jury's eyes already glazed with fatigue and conviction.

The defense calls no witnesses. Instead, the lawyer appeals to the jury's sense of fairness, invoking the "burden of proof" with the resignation of a man who knows the outcome is preordained. There is no drama, no last-minute revelation, no twist of fate to jolt the room into uncertainty.

Then, the bailiff calls the next witness: "Angelique King."

The air in the gallery crystallizes. Heads turn. A faint, collective gasp ripples through the seats.

Angelique stands, moving as if summoned from a trance. She walks the length of the courtroom, her footsteps muffled by the ugly brown carpet, and mounts the witness stand without looking at her brother. She is sworn in, voice steady but so quiet the clerk must ask her to repeat.

The prosecutor approaches, slow and careful, as if handling a live charge.

"Miss King, do you recall the evening of September fifteenth?"

Angelique nods.

"Where were you that night?"

She hesitates, just a moment. "Home. In my room."

"Who else was present in the home?"

She recites the list: "My mother, my father, my younger brother, my older brother. And Alphonse."

The prosecutor nods, waiting. "Did Alphonse leave the house that evening?"

"Yes."

"Did you see him return?"

A longer pause. "Yes."

"What time?"

"I don't know. Late. After midnight."

"And when he returned—what did you observe?"

Angelique's hands, beneath the ledge of the witness box, curl into fists. She stares at a fixed point on the table, voice barely audible.

"He had blood on his shirt. On his hands. He washed them in the bathroom."

The defense objects, but the judge waves it off. "Let her answer."

"Did you see anything else?" the prosecutor prompts.

Angelique nods, breath unsteady. "He had a gun. I saw it when he took off his jacket. He put it in a paper bag and left again."

The prosecutor leans in, just enough to catch her eye. "Can you say, for the record, whether that gun resembled the one in the evidence bag?"

Angelique looks at the plastic-shrouded weapon, then at her brother, and for the first time, meets his eyes.

"Yes," she says.

The room holds the silence, unwilling to let go.

On the defense table, Alphonse sits very still. His mouth works once, then closes. His eyes do not move, but something in the jawline falters. For the first time all morning, he looks his age.

The prosecutor thanks Angelique. She steps down, walking back to her seat without looking at anyone.

As she passes Alphonse, he whispers, so softly it is almost lost: "Blood thicker than water, huh?"

Angelique blinks, then keeps walking.

The jury deliberates for less than an hour.

Beth does not watch the verdict read. She closes her eyes, lips moving in silent prayer. Wilbur squeezes her hand, but his own trembles.

Alphonse stands as the judge announces the sentence: twenty years to life, with possibility of parole at the discretion of the court. His shoulders twitch forward then back, as if he might run or might collapse, before settling into a rigid line.

The bailiff reaches for his arm. Alphonse jerks away, then offers his wrists. The family watches, Beth's fingers whitening around her Bible, Wilbur's jaw working silently. Angelique half-rises from her seat before sinking back down.

Beth's first tear falls only after the doors have closed, darkening Psalm 37 where her thumb has worn the page thin. She wants to wipe it away but can't decide if she's crying for her son or for the man he killed.

Angelique sits apart, hands folded then unfolded, then folded again.

Outside, traffic lights change from red to green to red. Inside, nothing moves. Not for a long, long time.

The courthouse empties slowly, as if grief itself needs time to gather its coat and hat. The Kings linger in the echoing hallway; each caught in the undertow of separate thoughts.

Wilbur stands by the window, watching a city bus lumber away through morning fog, his silhouette framed in cold, flat light. Beth sits on a wooden bench, Bible closed, hands resting in her lap. She doesn't cry—her tears dried up somewhere between the verdict and the sound of the cell door latching shut. Her mind has already jumped ahead: commissary lists, letters she'll write that may never be answered, prayers she will repeat until she believes them again.

Angelique hovers near the exit, back pressed against the marble, waiting for something—absolution, maybe, or simply the courage to go home.

Wilbur turns, the lines on his face deepening. "We have to go," he says, but his voice carries no conviction.

Beth rises, smoothing her skirt, and touches Wilbur's arm. "He'll need us," she says softly, meaning Alphonse—but also herself, and all of them.

Angelique swallows hard, looking at her father for the first time. "I'm sorry," she whispers—not just for her testimony, but for everything that's broken.

Wilbur nods, pulling her into a brief, shaky embrace. "Family endures," he says, but the words feel like a wish more than a truth.

They file out together. On the courthouse steps, the city feels changed: brighter, sharper, emptied of mercy.

Beth pauses, glancing behind her at the courthouse doors, as if expecting Alphonse to emerge, smiling and whole. She squares her shoulders. "Let's go home," she says.

They walk off into the thin morning light, their shadows merging and pulling apart, searching for each other as the city stirs awake around them.

Down the block, the bells of Triumph Church ring out the hour, and the sound follows them—fragile, persistent, a reminder that there is life after sorrow, even if it must be rebuilt one day at a time.

Across town, the Red Chilie Peppers gather in a back room, whispering about fresh recruits and unfinished business. On a battered school playground, Manon runs in circles, too young to know what was lost.

The King family keeps moving forward, battered but unbroken, even as unseen storms gather on the horizon—preparing for the moment when the past will demand its reckoning, and the future will call them to account.

www.ingramcontent.com/pod-product-compliance
Lightning Source LLC
Chambersburg PA
CBHW060327260626
47160CB00007B/2703